The Adventures of Don Chipote
or
When Parrots Breast-Feed

Recovering the U.S. Hispanic Literary Heritage

Board of Editorial Advisors

The Adventures of Don Chipote
or
When Parrots Breast-Feed

Daniel Venegas

Translated from the Spanish by
Ethriam Cash Brammer

With a New Introduction by
Nicolás Kanellos

Recovering the U.S. Hispanic Literary Heritage

Arte Público Press
Houston, Texas
2000

Publication of this volume is made possible through generous support of the
Rockefeller Foundation, without whose support neither this volume nor the
Recovering the U. S. Hispanic Literary Heritage project would be possible.
Our grateful thanks to the foundation and especially to Tomás Ybarra-Frausto
and Lynn Swaja.

Recovering the past, creating the future

Arte Público Press
University of Houston
Houston, Texas 77204-2174

Cover design by Ken Bullock
Original art by Malaquías Montoya

Venegas, Daniel.
    [Aventuras de don Chipote. English]
    The adventures of don Chipote, or, When parrots breast-feed :
a novel / by Daniel Venegas; translation by Ethriam Cash Brammer.
    p.   cm.
    ISBN 1-55885-297-2 (pbk. : alk. paper)
    I. Title: Adventures of don Chipote. II. Title: When parrots
breast-feed. III. Brammer, Ethriam Cash. IV. Title.
PQ7079.2.V34 A9413 2000
863'.64 — dc21   00-023987
                                                                  CIP

♾ The paper used in this publication meets the requirements of the
American National Standard for Information Sciences—Permanence of
Paper for Printed Library Materials, ANSI Z39.48-1984.

0 1 2 3 4 5 6 7 8 9   0 9 8 7 6 5 4 3 2 1

Daniel Venegas

Contents

Introduction

The Adventures of Don Chipote, or, When Parrots Breast-Feed, first published by Los Angeles' Spanish-language daily newspaper *El heraldo de México* in 1928, must have represented an heroic effort to validate the life and experiences of Mexican immigrant workers in the United States at that time. For us today, Daniel Venegas' novel is one of the few vestiges of the creativity and social and political identity of "Chicanos" in the early twentieth century. No other document has been found which celebrates Chicano identity so openly or which provides such an incisive socio-political analysis of the precarious existence of Mexican laborers in the United States during that period. It is even more remarkable that this analysis was effected from within a literary genre: the picaresque novel. For today's reader, therefore, interest is twofold: first, as socio-historic testimony on the labor conditions, culture and expressive forms of the *braceros* at that time; second, as an early example of Mexican-American working-class literature. Venegas himself seems to have recognized these two, apparently contradictory, objectives in his novelistic project: writing a testimony based on historical experience and thus protesting the socio-economic conditions of Chicanos; creating a fictional narrative based on the idiomatic and cultural expression of Chicanos, with whom he not only sympathized but most certainly identified. The historical value of *Don Chipote* is at least matched by its importance as literature. In our hands we hold an extremely innovative literary document which attempts to accommodate a new theme and new characters within the tradition of picaresque literature and the epic road story, as exemplified by *Don Quijote*. Instead of Lazarillos and Don Quijotes, we now have the naive *campesino*, a greenhorn, if you will, in the grand metropolis, where he encounters acculturated Mexicans, renegades, flappers and a slew of bicultural Mexicans (Americans) arising from Mexican-American folkore.

There are innumerable passages in the novel which indicate that

1

Venegas wrote the novel for "Chicanos," that is, Mexican immigrant laborers or *braceros*. Not only did he incorporate their dialect and their folkore, but he repeatedly appealed directly to them in the narration: "Now, readers, here you have Don Chipote on his way to California. Will he make it? Those of you who have been hooked into working on the *traque*, tell me. Does he have much left to go?" (59) He also utilized the first-person plural, which included his narrator among the ranks of Chicanos: "We," "Our buddies," "We, the Chicanos." Thus, his ideal readers were "those of us who have set out for the infamous United States." (99) If Venegas was at all successful in his novelistic project, then *Don Chipote* is the first Chicano novel, the first to be directed to a Chicano readership—even if some of the readers were in reality *listeners*—listening to their literate companions, who would read aloud to the other *braceros* after a long day's work.

The Adventures of Don Chipote is an immigration novel that seems to have suddenly arisen from the rich wellsprings of oral tradition, where its basic plot already existed, as did the character types and even the specific argot of the Chicanos; all of these had made their way from the anecdotes and lived experience of the *bracero* immigrants into jokes, popular ballads (*corridos*) and vaudeville routines that became so popular in Mexican-American culture in the United States in the early twentieth century. The character types as well as their picturesque argot had developed in oral culture from at least the turn of the century, if not before, and broke into print first in the local-color columns (*crónicas*) of Spanish-language newspapers published throughout the Southwest. In the weekly *crónicas* of such satirists as "Jorge Ulica" (Julio B. Arce), "Kaskabel" (Benjamín Padilla),[1] "Loreley" (María Luisa Garza), "Az T. K." (pseudonym of an unknown author), "El Malcriado" (Daniel Venegas) and many others,[2] the customs of Mexican immigrants were habitually transformed into literary texts in accordance with the Mexican satirical traditions identified and studied by Carlos Monsiváis.[3] The written literature of immigration in the Spanish language was represented not just by the *crónicas*; there were also hundreds of books of immigrant literature issued by publishing houses and newspapers. Among these were many novels, including those written by such authors as Conrado Espinosa,[4] Miguel Arce[5] and Alirio Díaz Guerra,[6] who were inspired in the real-life epic of Hispanic immigration to the United States. For now, Díaz Guerra's *Lucas*

Guevara seems to be the first example of the novel of Hispanic immigration, having been published in New York in 1914. In this early novel are found many of the formulas which would be repeated in the novels to follow: 1) the young greenhorn immigrant arrives in the metropolis full of illusions of impending success; 2) he becomes the victim of an urban underworld, or of exploitation, and he loses his innocence; 3) he becomes disillusioned; 4) he returns to his homeland or he dies. Throughout the novel, the United States is contrasted with the homeland, which is idealized as pristine and honest, although unable to afford its native son with the education or economic resources to sustain an adequate level of existence. The United States, while seen as the seat of great industrial and technological progress, is also a center for corruption, racism and dehumanization—for Díaz Guerra, it is a modern Babylon. Beyond mere local color in these novels is the depiction of the social environment in the United States, which is uniformly portrayed as corrupt and anti-Hispanic. It is no coincidence that these formulas are also to be found in numerous *corridos*[7] and vaudeville reviews.[8] And they have persisted to the present in oral lore as well as such written works as René Marqués' *La carreta*, Iván Acosta's *El super* and Miguel Méndez's *Peregrinos de Aztlán*.

So far as the folk base of *Don Chipote* is concerned, there is a notable similarity between its plot of coming to the United States "to sweep the gold up from the streets" and that of several *corridos*, including *El lavaplatos*[9] (The Dishwasher), which besides coinciding in the narrative structure of immigrating and working on the *traque* (railroad), also coincides in the attraction that the cinema and theater hold for their respective protagonists, their progressive disillusionment (*"Adiós sueños de mi vida"*/Good-bye, my life's dreams) and their return to Mexico (*"vuelvo a mi patria querida/más pobre de lo que vine"*/ I return to my beloved fatherland/poorer than when I left). The message of *El lavaplatos* is just as clear and firm as that of *Don Chipote*: Mexicans should not come to the United States.

Qué arrepentido
qué arrepentido
estoy de haber venido.

Aquél que no quiera creer
que lo que digo es verdad,
Si se quiere convencer
que se venga para acá.

————————————

How regretful
how regretful
I am of having come.

He who won't believe
that what I say is true,
is sure to be convinced
by coming straight here.

The burlesque tone of *Don Chipote*, so characteristic of this *corrido* as well as of the *crónicas* that Daniel Venegas wrote, serves to entertain the reader and soften the criticism of the socio-economic-political reality on both sides of the border that led the poor to leave their homeland for "slave-drivers," *coyotes*, ladies of the night and flappers—all of whom are personifications of the hostile and corrupt metropolitan environment. Daniel Venegas' tragicomic treatment of immigration was developed during his years of writing and directing vaudeville reviews for the poorest classes of Mexican immigrants and of writing, illustrating and publishing his weekly satirical tabloid, *El Malcriado* (The Brat). Díaz Guerra, on the other hand, was a medical doctor and a poet who came from the privileged elite in Colombia. An intellectual and political activist, Díaz Guerra found his way to New York as a political exile, expelled from both Colombia and Venezuela. He avoided the kind of grass-roots humor characteristic of Venegas to explore the mythic dimensions of exile and "Babylonian captivity" in New York. While Venegas chose *Don Quijote* as a metatext, Díaz Guerra found his inspiration in the Bible. In *Don Chipote*, the flappers (acculturated but Mexican, after all) represent acculturation and dis-loyalty to the homeland; in *Lucas Guevara*, the Eves are the American temptresses, personifications of iniquitous Yankee culture, which lures the protagonist into perdition, after he has turned his back on Latin American religion and morality. While in *Don Chipote* social order is reestablished with Doña Chipota's rescue and return to Mexico of her straying husband—for she represents the hearth and home and Mexican family and cultural values—Díaz Guerra's Hispanic Everyman cannot be rescued, for there is no salvation possible after having given himself over completely to Eve. Lucas, thus, commits suicide by diving from the Brooklyn Bridge, a symbol at that time of Yankee technological and industrial prowess.[10]

One of the principal achievements of Daniel Venegas in *Don Chipote* is his detailing of the social environment of the *bracero* during the 1920s. Despite the strong influence of the picaresque literary tradition, Venegas provides a fascinating depiction of life on the streets of Juárez, El Paso and Los Angeles: from the boarding houses, whorehouses and cheap movie houses to the brutish work on the tracks and in hauling cement, from the working-class eateries to the fleabag hotels, from the relationship between foremen and laborers to the companies and their exploitive stores; from the rural dialect of the sharecroppers to the hybrid dialect of the urban workers in their historical effort to adjust to a foreign language and culture. Venegas' attention to local color, also perfected in his *crónicas,* makes the novel not only an important historical document but also one of those literary gems which succeed in revealing to the appreciative modern reader a world previously unknown. For the Chicano readers and listeners of the past, the faithful reflection of their daily lives must have had great emotional and intellectual impact.

On the other hand, Venegas' desire to historicize his narrative and document social reality led him to break the fictive artifice of his narration, repeatedly interjecting first-person testimony as to the injustice and oppression suffered by the immigrants—which the historical Daniel Venegas must have experienced at first hand—and to protest not only the mistreatment of Chicanos but the complicity of the governments of Mexico and the United States in their exploitation, which Venegas compares to slavery:

> In the border cities, El Paso among them, there exists a certain class of people who are Mexican and who devote themselves to taking advantage of the innocence of our countrymen. Without any scruples whatsoever, they become instruments for the companies and landowners, who, knowing that Mexican *braceros* can be useful in

> all types of work, put Mexicans in those recruitment office, drawing
> most of their employees from them, as frontmen or callers, who
> attend to shipping out greenhorns to the *traque* or the cotton fields,
> where the workers are usually treated like animals. Those slave dri-
> vers who make their living from Mexican disgrace . . . (52–53)

> . . . the foreman is the slave driver of the Mexican infidel whom he
> has do his bidding. He cares very little about the suffering of those
> who are so grateful to the company which employs them. (70)

Although the narrator begins and ends his tale with an obviously elitist
and burlesque attitude, and therefore establishes a certain distance
between himself and his characters, after the initial chapters and once
into the action he eliminates that distance in order to participate in the
story directly as an historical witness and commentator. While the
characters never escape their typology, the narrator himself becomes
another character, one who elicits our sympathy for Chipote's suffering
as well as our enmity for those who have exploited and mistreated him
and thousands of other real-life *bracero* immigrants. As the narrator
progressively identifies with his Chicano characters, he recalls unfor-
tunate episodes from his own "life"; as he and his characters become
more and more humanized, Venegas' ideological project is advanced.
For many literary critics this attempt to serve two masters—art and history—is undoubtedly an aesthetic mistake: Venegas sacrifices the
fictive and artistic project to document social history and make a political statement. Even the narrator recognizes the danger inherent in
these repeated documentary interruptions, and asks the forbearance of
the readers: "My readers will forgive me for introducing them . . ."
(117) But he, nevertheless, repeats these autobiographical interjections
despite declaring early on that he would leave history to the historians
or, at least to more "ingenious" and "long-winded" writers:

> It would be a very difficult task to present the life of Mexicans in the
> United States, and more importantly, we don't want to dig too deeply,
> so we leave that work to wordsmiths who are more ingenious and
> long-winded than we. If we have made this brief parenthesis and we
> have digressed from our tale, it is only to send the real character of
> this story, Don Chipote de Jesús María Domínguez, on his way.
> (28–29)

In these "parentheses," the "historicized" Daniel Venegas comes to usurp the first level of the narrative and wrests historicity away from Don Chipote and his companions. Without a doubt, the painful reality of abuse and injustice were more important to the author than the fictive world he was creating and populating with interesting characters, who in the final analysis were only comic inventions meant to entertain. Although *Don Chipote* may not be an accomplished work of literary art, we do have the extraordinary potential in this text of comparing the memories of an historical figure with their literary re-creation or re-elaboration. That is, the tragicomic plot—what Venegas is wont to call *"joco-seria"*—is the literary representation of the tragicomic biography of the author and thousands of his compatriots. And the implicit anonymity of the typical immigrant *bracero* Don Chipote—a name signifying a lump resulting from a blow to the head—is part of the author's intent to give the narrative an epic dimension: This is the story of the Chicanos, the *braceros* who immigrated to the United States.

In addition, *Don Chipote* is a text whose announced purpose is to illustrate why Mexicans should not come to the United States, that they should stay in Mexico and continue being Mexicans—even while in the United States. This objective was not new or innovative, given that the majority of intellectual refugees of the Mexican Revolution promoted an ideology of exile, which called for the protection and preservation of the mother culture and the mother tongue in anticipation of an ultimate return to Mexico. Both editorial writers and *cronistas* reinforced this ideology on a daily basis and warned against the adoption of Anglo-American customs. The *cronista* "Jorge Ulica" in particular severely censured the *campesinos* who were fascinated with everything "American" and, like Venegas' character Pitacio, sang the glories of U. S. culture, thus motivating the *campesinos* to abandon their homeland. Both Venegas and "Ulica" not only satirized the recently arrived greenhorns, who believed that everything American was superior to what was to be found at home, but they also unmercifully attacked the *"pochos," "agringados"* and *"renegados,"*[11] terms derogating Mexicans in various degrees of acculturation or assimilation, a process of course seen as treason by these *cronistas*. In *Don Chipote*, the attack on the *agringados* and *renegados* is one of the longest and most severe to be found in this protest novel:

I don't want to go any further without first providing a brief analysis of the weakness of some Mexicans who, like the guy approached by Policarpo, cross the border and forget how to speak their own language. Disgracefully, these people abound. And they, who have come to the United States with one hand covering the holes in their seats and the other looking for a handout, who like the majority of Mexican immigrants have suffered immeasurable mistreatment by our *gringo* cousins, doled out to those of us who work on the railroad, have forgotten even the parish in which their fat heads were anointed when they were baptized. They speak a few words of English and boast of being *gringos*, especially when they come across fellows who are fresh off the boat, to whom they brag about their knowledge of *tok inglis*. These people, like all Mexicans who live in search of work, have received infinite humiliations at the hands of foremen and have served as slaves to blacks, who, in order to keep the railroad companies happy and to maintain their employment, make our compatriots work like animals or worse.

However, these Mexicans become so conceited with the "fine" manners with which they are treated that not just a few have come to deny their fatherland without any more justification than that of having tried ham and eggs, which, it seems, makes them the worst thorn in the side of the Mexican *bracero*, who has come to this country in search of a piece of bread for his family.

Can there be any greater wickedness than that of these bastards who, passing as *gringos*, refuse to speak their own language, denying even the country in which they were born? I think not.

From these renegades—who are neither fish nor fowl, who speak neither Spanish nor English, who are, in a word, ignorant—is where the harshest epithets about us have come. So, then, all this talk about *cholos*, "greenhorns" and "dumb Mexicans" is reason for them to stick up their noses at the new arrivals from Mexico. (51)

Today we know that the target for much of this criticism was the Mexican American who was hired as the translator, intermediary and even the foreman. The bilingual-bicultural Mexican American considered himself superior to the poor, ragged, provincial Mexicans who came to the Southwest in desperate need of work. The *braceros*, on the other hand, resented their American cousins' economic advantage and sense of superiority, derived from their "Yankee know-how" and imprecise bilingualism. Resentment, thus, was expressed in a nationalist reaction which consisted in seeing the Mexican Americans as unfaithful, as traitors, as renegades of Mexican nationality. What many of the newly arrived did not understand was that many of these *"pochos"* were not denying their homeland; because they in fact were born and/or raised in the United States; and that moreover they had also been subjected—and were still subjected—to discrimination because of their language, ethnicity or color. Thus, the target in *Don Chipote* is not only the Anglo-American and his land of supposed opportunity and democracy, but also every Mexican who allows himself to be deceived by this American dream, who abandons his country and nationality and motivates others to do the same.

Although the moral of the book—that Mexicans will never become wealthy in the United States—is aimed at "Mexicans," and although the book is culturally nationalistic especially in its attack on acculturated Mexican Americans, it is obvious that Venegas is purveying a working-class perspective. Venegas' characters are rural and urban laborers, not Mexicans of all social classes. Although Venegas certainly knew and worked daily with middle-class and wealthy Mexicans in his life as a writer, editor and vaudeville director, his alter ego-narrator in *Don Chipote* (as well as in his newspaper *El Malcriado*) identifies with the working-class Chicanos, with their values, their struggle against exploitation and the abuses of the foremen, the contractors, the company store and those who take advantage of the greenhorns. More than that, the author has created a style based on the workers' oral tradition, dialect, sense of humor (mostly physical and low humor), sense of community, family and religion. The resultant product may be considered the first "Chicano" novel—or, at least, a precursor to the Chicano novel of the 1960s and 1970s, which also identifies with the working class, albeit the *Mexican-American* working class. Chicano literature of the 1960s and 1970s, of course, was written by Mexican American authors who, for the most part, were born or raised in the United States. In *their* cultural nationalist scheme, it is interesting to note, the treacherous "renegade" has evolved into the *vendido* or sellout,[12] and today's Chicano is not an immigrant but a working-class Mexican American.

While Daniel Venegas' social and political stance appears to be "liberal" and "progressive" in defending the rights and culture of Mexican workers, that stance does not appear to have included women, even when the women in his writings are workers themselves. In *Don*

Chipote, each of the working "gals," whether waitresses, vaudeville performers or prostitutes, is satirized severely. The sole purpose of their existence in the novel is to take advantage of Don Chipote and the other greenhorns. Don Chipote's flapper waitress plays him for a sucker, the prostitute who barges into his fleabag hotel in Juárez steals his cash, and the vaudeville actress makes her living by showing skin; they are all personifications of the hostile and corrupt environment of the United States (yes, even in the border city of Juárez). Venegas does not include them among the ranks of Chicanos nor show them any of the endearment and regard that he displays for working-class males. In *El Malcriado* as well, Venegas satirizes the poor waitresses in their worn-out, malodorous shoes as they struggle to make a living in Los Angeles.[13] That Venegas was writing for Chicano males is explained, in part, by the historical reality that the first waves of economic refugees of the Mexican Revolution were predominantly males and that women were not contracted for work on the railroad and cement mixing and other hard labor portrayed in *Don Chipote*. The narrator in the novel glosses on the absence of women in railroad work, especially felt when the men have to cook and care for themselves:

> For those men who have never stirred a pot in Mexico before coming to the United States, the culinary crisis is their first tribulation, for while working on the *traque*, each one has to prepare his own meals or go hungry. So, since there is no greater wax than that which burns, and since the stomach knows no etiquette, there is no solution other than to fix one's own chow. But, since back in Mexico most of us are attended by our old ladies just because we're men, it just so happens that here in the desert, where we don't have anyone to do these things for us, the first thing we do is cry—because of all the smoke. (67-68)

There is no doubt in Venegas' mind that a woman's place was in the home, and it is therefore Doña Chipota's express task to represent the nuclear family and religious and patriotic values in her rescue of Don Chipote from perdition in the United States. Doña Chipota's odyssey, consequently, serves to precipitate the novel's climax and resolve the plot; it is *she* who reestablishes social order by returning this particular Mexican to Mexico. Although her assertiveness and valor may remove her somewhat from the stereotypical literary mother, she is, in fact, the saintly contrast to the flappers and prostitutes, the Virgin Mary to their Eve.

In the culture of exile constructed by the Mexican immigrants, it was necessary to preserve Mexican culture, language, values and customs in an environment seen as foreign and aggressively hostile. This included preserving the gender roles as they were constituted in Mexico. The large outpouring of Mexican immigrants into the United States occurred during a period of liberalization of gender roles in the United States; women's rights were expanding, as was a woman's acceptable public sphere of action. In the midst of this liberalization, some of the most inflexible segments of Mexican society were introduced into the United States as political and religious refugees. The economic refugees from the provinces also represented traditional Mexican values. The first reaction of both economic and political refugees to American's liberalization of gender roles was not to embrace it but to exert greater control over their women. Mexican men perceived the potential for a comparatively advantageous position for Mexican women in the social hierarchy in the United States: Not only were there fewer Mexican women available in exile, but there was competition from Anglo-American males, who practiced more liberal treatment of women. Daniel Venegas, "Jorge Ulica" and many other *cronistas* were attempting to promote more social control over women through their writings not only by criticizing women working outside the home but also by showing how they were more likely to acculturate and further the loss of Mexican nationality.[14] These writers made *women* responsible for the survival of the group in exile; it was up to *women* to keep the family united, to raise the children as Mexicans and as Catholics, and to maintain the use of Spanish and protect the family circle from the invasion of Anglo-American values and practices, which were seen as morally and ethically corrupt.

The Life of Daniel Venegas

We know very little about Daniel Venegas' life. What little information we have comes from three sources: the sole remaining issue of his newspaper *El Malcriado*, newspaper reviews of his theatrical works and the autobiographical passages in *The Adventures of Don Chipote*. Emerging from these sources is the image of a man of letters, albeit a street-wise intellectual, who was very knowledgeable of Mexican working-class life, especially in the Mexican communities in Los Angeles and El Paso.

Venegas' name appears in the Spanish-language press of Los Angeles, primarily in reviews of his plays and of his vaudeville ensemble Compañía de Revistas Daniel Venegas, between 1924 and 1933. His theatrical group always seemed to perform in the more modest, working-class houses of the city. This was not always so for the production of his (now lost) plays. *¿Quién es culpable?* (Who Is to Blame?) had its debut in 1924; *Nuestro egoísmo* (Our Selfishness), a three-act play, debuted in 1926 and was written "in honor and defense of Mexican women," according to *El Heraldo de México*, October 11, 1926; of the play *Esclavos* (Slaves, 1930), we can only speculate that its theme related to Mexican labor;[15] and his vaudeville reviews included *El maldito jazz* (That Darned Jazz); *Revista astronómica* (The Astronomic Review); *El establo de Arizmendi* (Arizmendi's Stable), which celebrated the famed Mexican boxer Baby Arizmendi; and the supposedly very popular *El con-su-la-do* (a play on the word "consulate" in Spanish). While these later works were of the musical comedy variety so enjoyed by blue-collar audiences, it is almost certain that *¿Quién es culpable?* and *Nuestro egoísmo* were works of drama, especially since the "first lady" of the Mexican theater, Virginia Fábregas, produced both for the stage in Los Angeles. Notwithstanding this distinction, *Nuestro egoísmo*'s debut during a play-writing contest was severely criticized by the jury as well as theater critic and fellow playwright Gabriel Navarro for its "*libertad de lenguaje*," which we might interpret as foul language according to the criteria of the times (*El heraldo de México*, June 1, 1928). Could, however, this "*libertad de lenguaje*" have been working-class dialect?

From 1924 to 1929, Daniel Venegas wrote, edited and published a weekly satirical newspaper, *El Malcriado* (The Brat), which poked fun at the customs of and politics in the Mexican community of Los Angeles. Venegas himself came to be known as "El Malcriado," for his penchant for taking jabs at community figures through his newspaper. His talent for burlesque was also evident in the cartoons that he drew to illustrate the stories in his tabloid. Before founding *El Malcriado*, Venegas had worked for the *El pueblo* newspaper in Los Angeles and, because *El heraldo de México* published his *Don Chipote*, he may have been a staff writer for that paper as well. There is no information available as to whether Venegas had any formal education or newspaper experience in Mexico before emigrating to the United States.

The April 7, 1927, issue of *El Malcriado* is the only one that has been located to date. Its ten pages are filled with satirical entries on sports, entertainment, and current and world events, accompanied by cartoons. Of literary interest is Venegas' penchant for adopting various dialects in the news items, editorials and short fiction contained in his tabloid. The majority of the burlesque is conducted in a style very similar to that used in *Don Chipote*, including the use of Chicano dialect. This is not the case in the paper's editorial, which is written in standard, professional Spanish, and is directed to the members of the Mexican Journalists Association of California, which Venegas served as president. It is apparent from this editorial that Venegas subscribed to the attitude, common among Mexican intellectuals in the United States, that it was the duty of journalists, writers and artists to preserve Mexican culture in exile:

> The journalists and their association should become the leaders of the Mexican organizations as guides towards a future of active solidarity and true patriotism among all of the exiles.
> That is, to achieve dignity not only for Mexican workers in a foreign land—the journalists are also workers—but for the homeland, in a very special way.

Through the example of his prose, however, both in the satirical columns and in his novel, Venegas was not furthering the expected defense of Mexican culture that he extols in this editorial: His literary pen was full of Anglicisms, neologisms and popular dialects, which became part of the basis for his unique style. This lexical display was anathema to many of the other Mexican writers and journalists in the

United States. For them, this style of writing represented something akin to surrender to the enemy instead of protecting the language of Cervantes.

Without a doubt, the discovery in the future of Venegas' lost plays or of other issues of *El Malcriado* will reveal further similarities to *Don Chipote*. The structure of the individual chapters in the novel seems to indicate that they were originally published in serial form in a newspaper. Could they have appeared first in *El Malcriado*? Perhaps this mystery, as well as those of the author's biography and the whereabouts of his other literary works, will be solved in the future.

A Note on the Research

The Adventures of Don Chipote was a previously unknown work. I had never imagined that such a work existed; neither the newspapers of the time nor the most important archives of Hispanic materials in the United States recorded this title. I began learning of Daniel Venegas when, during the 1970s and 1980s, I was looking for dramatic works in preparation for my *History of Hispanic Theater in the United States, Origins to 1940* (University of Texas Press, 1990). Around 1978, I found mention of Venegas' theatrical works and an interview of the author in the pages of Los Angeles' *El heraldo de México* and *La opinión*. I thus added Venegas to my list of some fifty playwrights whose works I would research in the catalogs and archives of all of the libraries and collections I visited, from New York to Los Angeles, from Spain to Puerto Rico and Mexico. Among the papers of Mexican sociologist Manuel Gamio, archived at the Bancroft Library of the University of California at Berkeley, I chanced upon an uncataloged issue of a satirical newspaper: Daniel Venegas' weekly *El Malcriado*. During the many years of my research project, I was able to find many plays (the majority of them unpublished) and many non-dramatic works of these playwrights, but not a single vestige of Venegas' works. Finally, in the newly reorganized card catalog of the National Library of Mexico Daniel Venegas appeared as the author of their holding *Las aventuras de Don Chipote, o Cuando los pericos mamen*. On examining the book, I immediately recognized its value and took a photocopy with me to show my friend and colleague Jorge Bustamante, a sociologist at the Colegio de México. Bustamante agreed with my assessment of the novel's importance and jokingly warned that I could not leave the country with "national patrimony." But, I protested, *Don Chipote* had been written and published in Los Angeles in 1928; at a minimum, it was binational patrimony. Bustamante persisted and insisted that *Don Chipote* see the light of day again first in Mexico; he thus arranged for its publication, with my introduction, by the Secretariat of Education and his own research center, CEFNOMEX, in 1985. When the work appeared in Mexico, the reviews were unanimously positive, and frequently expressed surprise at its linguistic and cultural vitality; the critics had never encountered such a work.

A few years ago, that first new edition of twenty thousand sold out. This past year the Recovering the U. S. Hispanic Literary Heritage project has issued a new Spanish-language edition and now this, the first English translation of an Hispanic novel of immigration.

Nicolás Kanellos
University of Houston

Notes

[1] Padilla published two collections of *crónicas*; among are to be found many signed by "Kaskabel," written during his exile in the United States: *Un puñado de artículos: filosofía barata*, 2nda edición (Barcelona: Casa Editorial Maucci, s.d.); and *Otro puñado de artículos* (Guadalajara, 1913).

[2] Various studies have appeared over the years; nevertheless, a more consistant effort must be made to collect the *crónicas* of all of the principal writers. See Eleuteria Hernández, "La representación de la mujer mexicana en los EEUU en las *Crónicas Diabólicas* de Jorge Ulica," *Mester* 12/2 (Fall, 1993): 31-38; Clara Lomas, "Resistencia cultural o apropiación ideológica: Visión de los años 20 en los cuadros costumbristas de Jorge Ulica," *Revista Chicano-Riqueña* 6/4 (otoño, 1978): 44-49; Juan Rodríguez, "Jorge Ulica y Carlo de Medina: escritores de la Bahía de San Francisco," *La palabra* 2/1 (primavera, 1980): 25-47; Juan Rodríguez, *Crónicas diabólicas de "Jorge Ulica"/Julio B. Arce* (San Diego: Maize Press, 1982); Nicolás Kanellos, "Un relato de Azteca (Bromeando)," *Revista Chicano-Riqueña* 1/1 (1973): 5-8; Nicolás Kanellos, "Brief History/Overview of Spanish-language Newspapers in the United States," *Recovering the U.S. Hispanic Literary Heritage*, Volume I, eds. Ramón Gutiérrez and Genaro Padilla (Houston: Arte Público Press, 1993): 107-28; Nicolás Kanellos, "*Cronistas* and Satire in Early Twentieth-Century Hispanic Newspapers," *Melus* 23/1 (Spring, 1998) 3-25.

[3] *A ustedes les consta: Antología de la crónica en México* (México, D.F.: Ediciones Era, 1980).

[4] *El sol de Texas* (San Antonio: Viola Novelty Company, 1927).

[5] *¡Ladrona!* 2nda edición (San Antonio: Casa Editorial Lozano, 1925).

[6] *Lucas Guevara* (Nueva York: York Printing Company, 1914).

[7] See Arhoolie Records, "Texas-Mexican Border Music" series: "El corrido del lavaplatos" and "El Deportado" in Volume 2; "La Discriminación" in Volume 14; and jokes in Américo Paredes, *Uncle Remus con chile* (Houston: Arte Público Press, 1993).

[8] See Nicolás Kanellos, "Of Revistas, Comics and Composers," *A History of Hispanic Theatre in the United States: Origins to 1940*

(Austin: University of Texas Press, 1990): 59-70.

[9] See Arhoolie, "Texas-Mexican Border Music," Volume 14.

[10] This suicide has the same emotional and ideological charge as the death of Luis in the belly of a machine, again a symbol of technology, in René Marqués' *La carreta.*

[11] All three types were represented in folkore well before they appeared in written literature. See, for example, Netty and Jesús Rodríguez's recorded vaudeville routine, "Cabrestea o se ahorca," Arhoolie, Volume 14; also Romualdo Tirado's song from the vaudeville stage, among whose verses is the sentiment, "There is nothing so disgusting [*asqueroso*] as the degraded figure of the renegade," in Kanellos, *A History of Hispanic Theatre in the United States*, pp. 62-3.

[12] See, for example, Luis Valdez's "The Shrunken Head of Pancho Villa" and the Teatro de la Esperanza's "La víctima" in *Necessary Theater: Five Plays of the Chicano Experience*, ed. Jorge Huerta (Houston: Arte Público Press, 1989).

[13] See the one surviving issue of *El Malcriado*, in the appendix to the Spanish-language edition of *Las aventuras de Don Chipote, o Cuando los pericos mamen*, ed. Nicolás Kanellos (Houston: Arte Público Press, 1999).

[14] See Kanellos, *"Cronistas* and Satire in Early Twentieth Century Hispanic Newspapers," *Melus* 23/1 (Spring, 1988): 3-25.

[15] On the debut of *Esclavos*, the January 8, 1930 *La opinión* stated, "The author enjoys the support of the Mexican working-class of Los Angeles, and thus will surely have a full house tonight."

Translator's Acknowledgments

This translation could not have been realized without the help and support of numerous colleagues and friends. In particular, I thank Dr. Nicolás Kanellos for giving me this opportunity, by putting his faith in a graduate student—and an unproven translator—to work on a project very near to his heart. I also thank Dr. Carolyn Tipton for introducing me to the theories and techniques of literary translation and for encouraging me to pursue translation as a way of contributing to the world of literature. Next, I would like to express my appreciation to my dear friends Pier and Catherine Parisio for use of their personal computer, without which I might never have finished the manuscript. Similarly, I am grateful for the kind support of Sister Adriana Rebeca Zuro and the faculty and staff of Vincent Memorial High School for the use of their printing and copying facilities. Finally, I thank my loving parents, Danny and Maria Brammer, for a lifetime of support and encouragement, and for providing me with the opportunity to return home and dedicate myself entirely to my writing.

Ethriam Cash Brammer

1

The sun vanished into the twilight as the clouds cloaked themselves in rouge upon receiving the caress of the blanket of the poor; and, like a lady of the night, they changed from red to black, resembling the exaggerated black eyes of starving clowns.

Loving flocks gathered in their nests, gave welcoming pecks, fluffed their wings, and prepared to snore. Bumblebees ceased buzzing; pumpkin blossoms puckered to pass the night; honeybees returned to the hive to puke up the honey they had swallowed; and the brook continued to sing and run its course while soaking the roots of the avocado, *camichime,* and *zalate* trees.

All was peace and calm. All of nature had entered into a state of respite, except for poor Don Chipote, who, completely worn out from the daily grind, continued to poke at an ox's ass. So obliged by his numerous progeny, he was forced to bring up the rear of his horny beast, occasionally sucking in the consoling little emanations from the animal's posterior duct.

Poor Don Chipote, at noontime, after polishing off the tacos he carried as provisions and sucking down a hand-rolled cigarette, was half-asleep and laid himself down to rest on a pile of corncobs; he dreamt that the cornfields, rather than ears of corn, yielded a harvest studded with glittering gold coins, and he felt downright extraordinary because now he would no longer need to work.

Dreams, only dreams—because, of the little he had planted, half was devoured by crows and the other half was left to be shared among his numerous progeny, the dog, the cat, and the herd.

It was getting dark, and Don Chipote and his oxen, feeling the tranquillity which comes after having worked till you can't work no more, set down the trail which led to the shadowy space beneath his home, all the while pondering his dreadful luck.

The barking of Skinenbones snapped him out of his meditations and made him realize that he was in front of his shack, where Doña

21

Chipota, his little Chipotitos, the cat, and Skinenbones waited for him so they could begin to gobble down supper.

After removing the yoke from the oxen and placing green blinders over their eyes (so they would eat the wood shavings he gave them instead of real feed), he went into the shanty. After greeting his ball-and-chain and shooting the terrified look of a sacrificial lamb at the calabash bowl filled with *gordas,* he cleaned the snot from his children's noses. Presently, having an appetite which made him feel as though he were hog-tied, he began to cram his face with dinner in the presence of his family—I mean "dinner" if one can call a puddle with three beans, a mortar of chili sauce, a jug of *atole,* and some tortillas "dinner." Nevertheless, for a good long while nothing could be heard but the thundering of teeth and the savoring sounds emitted from the receptacle tubes sucking down the food.

When Don Chipote's belly had been more or less satisfied, he asked his consort, "So how's yer mama's donkey?"

"Just swell. They sent word that she's dropped a baby mule," she responded.

"Who'da figgered?" answered Don Chipote. "After all this time believin' she was ready fer the glue factory an' all those urges had done left her, she goes an' drops a colt, with one foot awready in the grave. Well, at least now we've got another beast to work in the fiel', that is, a'course, if yer mama offers."

A grunt was Doña Chipota's only reply, at which Don Chipote, cleaning the thick barbs which served as his mustache, rose to have a smoke and wait till it was time to pray the rosary, something which, like good Christians, they never failed to do before sprawling out on their sleeping mat to await the morning and return to the daily grind.

2

Let's leave Don Chipote and family, sleeping naked as jaybirds, spread-eagle and snoring like there's no tomorrow, and turn our attention to some distance from his shack.

On the road leading to the ranchería, a native by the name of Pitacio advances with tired steps. The fact that he is walking at night doesn't mean that he is in a hurry to arrive; on the other hand, he does have his reasons for coming home after all the village's inhabitants have hit the hay.

But before going any further, we have the pleasure of presenting our character.

Pitacio, as we have said before, was originally born in the ranchería where our veridical story begins. Of poor yet drunk parents, the boy demonstrated a terrible fear of work from a very early age; for all the times that Pitacio's father sent him out to scare away the birds so they would not eat the crops, he had yet to get Pitacio to obey.

With such a prodigious beginning, Pitacio was not able to reach adulthood without having first buried his parents who were by then just about fed up with him; even so, he cried and felt the same emotions anyone feels when one's parents shove off from this world for the next.

Not to shirk the truth, however, we'll just say that if Pitacio was hurt by the loss of his progenitors, it was not so much because he was made an orphan; what hurt him most was that, upon burying his father, he was left without anyone to care for him. So, as we have already said, the poor boy didn't have even those good graces. It was then, after the casket raised his father to the clouds, that he thought about working at something in order to be able to quiet his belly. So without considering that he was an orphan, he began to scrounge for food.

Like they always say, "He who has never been a shepherd and suddenly tends sheep is not worth a darn." Pitacio, who had never been *prevented* from working, who had never earned a single tortilla

23

by the sweat of his brow, was turned away by all the villagers due to the simple fact that he did not pull his own weight.

This is how things went for a few months: He worked for all the sharecroppers in the vicinity, and they all fired him. Finally, as everyone is well aware, he had no other recourse than to set out for other parts where they did not know him.

It happened just like that: On a day like any other, good old Pitacio, after tying a hobo bundle with his little paws, was in the *ranchería* when night fell, but was gone by day break. And the sun came out to greet him a few leagues distant from the place where he had issued his first calf's cry when his dear mother had plopped him down in this vale of tears.

Where was Pitacio going? We don't know. And we can even be sure that he didn't know either. He only knew one thing: He was looking for work. That's how, then, while trotting his trot down the road, he distanced himself from his paternal home, thinking about how much he needed his parents.

Now as night fell, when his pedals began to go on strike and he was hungry enough to eat a horse, he spied from afar the town of Nacatécuaro. Seeing it and beginning to run were one and the same; the poor sap, not withstanding that he didn't have two pennies to rub together, believed that he was going to find a table set just for him in Nacatécuaro.

His race soon appeared to be crowned with victory; and, before the blanket of the poor submerged beneath the horizon, with belabored steps he entered the city, which to him, who knew nothing outside his *rancho,* looked like a great metropolis . . .

Not to give Pitacio more importance than he's worth, with a single stroke we will plant him in the United States, in a town in the state of Texas, where he had arrived after thousands of misfortunes, but where he, thanks to his damn gullet, could be found working. But after spending all that he made within a few days, and without anything left over for savings, with a little change Pitacio had salvaged, he managed to buy a dime-store suit of who knows how many hand-me-down generations, but which fit him very nicely.

The suit was not of a very high quality, except that it was of the cry-babiest baby-blue color that one could find and had buttons all over. In addition, our good Pitacio also bought himself the loudest bugle-blowing yellow shoes, silk stockings, and a cowboy hat.

In such trappings—and leaving the remaining eighty percent up to the imagination—even though no one would see him, since it was night and he wouldn't run into anyone on the street, we find Pitacio trotting down the road, drawing closer with each step to the *rancho* where he was born, precisely when we left Don Chipote and family surrendered to sleep.

Okay then, now that we have returned to the starting point, by means of our sovereign caprice, we go forward in time as we also push Pitacio forward up to the first barnyards in the *ranchería*.

It's five in the morning. The sun, once more like the day before, begins to emerge for the poor as much as for the rich. The little birds who spent the night beak to beak begin to leave their nests and go out to look for something or someone to peck.

The oxen expel air and occasionally bellow, not so much for the pleasure of the new day as for the sadness of thinking that the hour draws near when they must put on their yoke and pull a plow or cart.

The town's inhabitants, as much animals as the oxen, but reasoning animals, also take their last stretch on top of their mattressless floor mats; they indulge their last irresistible impulses; and they get up to prepare themselves to continue with the tasks which they left from the day before.

The morning is extremely beautiful: All of nature seems to have put on its prom dress to greet Pitacio, the prodigal son who returns home when his countrymen least expect it.

In Don Chipote's house, they too had thrown off their *sarapes;* and presently, Doña Chipota, Don Chipote's faithful companion, was nagging about mixing the *nixtamal* to later make the *tortillas gordas* that they would eat for lunch as well as those that her husband would take as provisions while he gave the livestock their slop. The dogs, headed by Skinenbones, began to bark outrageously at Pitacio, who could now be seen behind the pickets which divided the house's patio from the street.

The novelty of hearing the dogs bark must have been tremendous for the owners of the house, especially because the dogs, even when hungry, never barked, they doubtlessly being accustomed to all of the neighbors. That's why Don Chipote and his faithful companion stopped what they were doing and went outside to see who this person was for whom the dogs raised so much Cain. How great was their surprise upon butting into Pitacio, lazy Pitacio who everybody knew and who had now become an unrecognizable shell in that monkey suit which from a distance appeared to be far too soup-and-fish for their *rancho.*

It just goes to show you that clothes really do make the man. Pitacio, before being ordered to leave this place, had never been invited into anyone's home. But, on this occasion, as soon as they saw him dressed to the nines, Don Chipote as well as the missus believed him to be a person of great import, and with thousands of kind words they asked him in.

This being how he received his hand-outs—because he never begged—Pitacio took princely steps when entering the Chipote's humble abode. He headed directly for the kitchen, for what mattered to him most at that moment was that they would offer him lunch, since he had not put a scrap into his stomach since the previous day.

Don Chipote did not delay the invitation; in a few short moments, they were already gagging on boiled beans with their respective complements of hot sauce and warm *gordas.*

For a long while, they did not open their mouths except to take bites. And the good Doña Chipota was hard-pressed, with so much back and forth, behind this one then that one, to provide them with a steady supply of *gordas.*

Finally, when their bellies had now reached the breaking point, they took their respective papers and rolled themselves a smoke. They lit the cigarettes with a still burning stick. With a drag hanging from the point of his chin, Don Chipote asked Pitacio how he had accomplished converting himself into such a distinguished young gentleman.

Everyone knows that the laziest people have the biggest mouths, and Pitacio, who could win a prize in both categories, let his tongue fly and said: "Well, Don Chipote, sir. You know that my pop, may his soul rest in peace, was a very well-read and educated man, and I, his son, of course larned everything he had ta teach and maybe even a bit more. As you'll recall, I didn't like to go poking 'round ox asses cuz fer that ya don't needs no 'telligence, and I, who has vast 'mounts of knowledge, looked fer a way of makin' a livin' by the use of my mind. As you'll also remember, no one from the *rancho* or its surroundings ever understood me, and one by one they threw me out of their homes, until I saw that I was obliged to leave fer other parts where they could 'preciate my 'telligence.

"One day, as you'll recollect, I was at the rancho when night fell but was gone by daybreak, and I didn't stop until I reached the United States, the land of the white folk, which one really needs to see to believe.

"Oh, Don Chipote, if you could only see how sharp them people is over there! They really is smart and well-read, not like the parish priest here who is the most 'telligent in these parts. Not to draw out the story, because in the end there are things that you can only believe after seeing them with your own eyes, let me tell you that all the *gringos* appreciated me for what I was worth right from the get-go."

"So jus' how much did they pay fer ya?" asked Don Chipote.

"Don't be an ass," contested Pitacio. "They didn't buy me. I mean, they noticed right off that I too was a 'telligent person and they appointed me to a position where I earned three of those dollars which are worth twice as much as ours."

"An' which uns are those?" inquired Don Chipote, slobbering all over himself upon hearing such things.

"Well, they're the pesos from over there," said Pitacio, continuing. "You should know that *gringo* pesos are worth twice as much as the ones from here, so when somebody gets a dollar from over there, it's like making two of the ones from here."

"Ya don't say," said Don Chipote, going from wonder to absolute amazement. "An' ya say that ya were lucky enough to earn three a these?"

"Jus' like I told ya."

"So that means ya made six of ourn?"

"*Seguro que* yes."

"What do ya mean *yes?*" asked Don Chipote with his mouth opening wider and wider.

"Oh, *esquisme!*" said Pitacio. "I forgot that you don't speak any *toq inglis,* and here I am speaking to you in it. Well, see," he continued, "*yes* means the same thing as if we were to say *sí* in our tongue."

"*Caramba!*" burst out Don Chipote. "Ya really are some kinda bigshot now, aren't ya? Well, well, well, go on, keep tellin' me all 'bout these things. Let's see if'n I kin larn somethin'."

"What do ya wanna larn 'bout? There ain't nothin' ta larn 'bout!"

interrupted Doña Chipota, who up to that moment had kept quiet. "Now what do ya wan' him ta tell ya 'bout? How 'bout he tells you how he done git all the way over there? Better still, how 'bout ya go to this land of *güeros* an' make yerself a bigshot too?"

"That would be fabulous," agreed Pitacio.

"Ya think so?" replied Don Chipote.

"All you have to do is make up your mind to do it, an' you'll see right away what it means to suck the nectar from the tree of life . . ."

And that damned Pitacio, knowing that his tales assured him steady meals for the next few days, continued to tell thousands of lies that ended up trapping Don Chipote like a fox.

Of course, it never occurred to him to talk about the days and the nights that he went hungry, nor did he mention all the abuses the bosses had made him suffer while working on the *traque,* which is the fate of he who he has been so brilliantly deceived.

The United States is full of these Pitacios. Allow me to take the place of that egotistical man and talk of all of his lies, in order to tell you that every fellow countryman experiences bad luck when going up North; but instead of returning to his own great land to tell the God's honest truth about what happened, he twists it around when he returns, recounting stories to others and riling up all those that will listen.

Unfortunately, Chicanos appear to be born yesterday and enthusiastically believe everything one tells them about the North, and it is for this reason, more than the poor conditions in which the Revolution has left the country, that more and more people emigrate each day.

We don't want to deny that a few compatriots may have made something of themselves in the United States, but they, like a needle in a haystack, are the minority. But the majority go to the United States only to waste all of their energy, get abused by the foremen and humiliated by that country's citizens, so that, as soon as our countrymen reach old age, they are denied even the right to work in order to feed their own children.

It would be a very difficult task to truly present the life of Mexicans in the United States, and more importantly, we don't want to dig too deeply, so we leave that work to wordsmiths who are more ingenious and long-winded than are we. If we have made this brief parenthesis and we have digressed from our tale, it has only been to send the real character of the story, Don Chipote de Jesús María Domínguez, on his way.

Therefore, excusing all that was said before, so as not to lose the narrative thread, we shall place a final period, as we cast the spool of thread forward.

3

It was hopeless. Don Chipote had swallowed everything that Pitacio had told him—hook, line and sinker. For ten days he accommodated Pitacio just to hear about his adventures in the land of Uncle Sam; and during that same time, he failed to tend to the parcel of land that produced his food.

All of this made him think that if Pitacio—who all of his life had been a good-for-nothing bum, who had never worked a day in his life, who spent so many years poking at an ox's ass—had made himself into such a refined gentleman, then he was certain to make himself a millionaire over there before the cock crowed. And the more Don Chipote thought about it, the less he wanted to yoke the animals and tend to his plot of land that for so many years had provided him with food, though only beans and *gordas*. And the more he thought about it, the more the idea of going to the United States stuck in his head.

"I'm a goin'," he told his old lady. "I'm a goin' ta bring back all of de gold that they got over there. But before makin' my way back, I'll send fer ya so ya kin see that there land."

Doña Chipota was upset. But at the thought of the good fortune which awaited them, she agreed to the departure.

That poor gal, a woman after all, had also been enchanted by Pitacio's yarns; and, though anticipating the pain of separation, also encouraged Don Chipote, figuring that before long she would be seen wearing skirts and putting pins in her hair. She would be found hanging from her husband's arm, all fancied up and wearing a bowler hat, strolling down the streets of the United States.

After much deliberation and debate, the voyage was passed by the assembly with a majority of votes, all the Chipote relatives having taken part in the plebiscite. So they began the preparations for the journey.

Pitacio remained in charge of the management of the farm and, giving his word of honor, stayed to care for and maintain the family.

Because Don Chipote did not have much clothing, Doña Chipota made him another pair of underwear and another shirt out of a sheet; and, using him as a dummy, she fitted each item to his specifications. Likewise, Don Chipote sold a hog he had been fattening in order to buy himself some pants. And thus they furnished him as well as they could.

Doña Chipota did not give her grindstone a moment's rest when preparing his provisions. She quickly made him tacos with beans and quesadillas stuffed with pumpkin flowers and cheese. She fixed him a few small *gordas* with lard. In the end, all of her culinary ingenuity went to brighten the preparation of his knapsack. When all was ready, he announced his departure for the following morning. That night, when praying the rosary, the Chipote family offered up prayerful petitions to their patron saint and entrusted Don Chipote to all of the Heavenly Host. Husband and wife passed the night in tears and embraces.

In the morning they gave each other a final hug. Don Chipote cried with snot hanging down from his nose, and even Skinenbones let out a howl.

Later, when the sun began to remove the blackness from the clouds, when they blushed like a virgin who enters into the *zorra*-trot or fox-trot for the very first time and feels like she is dancing much too close—later, as we were saying, on the labyrinthine road, Don Chipote's humble figure marched double-time, carrying an enormous knapsack filled with more *gordas* than clothing. Skinenbones, who had decided to not separate himself from his master, followed him at a trot. They walked for long hours and their legs began to tremble. Why? Because Don Chipote had lost his appetite, absorbed in his thoughts and still saddened by the painful farewell. But he knew that Skinenbones was about to jump on him and stare at him with those puppy-dog eyes, so he decided to take a break to gorge himself with something his beloved consort had prepared for him. Just like that, then, he put his plan into action; and after making their way to the bend in the road, master and dog began to devour their first quesadillas.

The fatigue and stuffing themselves on the quesadillas made Don Chipote and his faithful Skinenbones feel too bloated to continue walking. And since night was falling upon them and they had more time than energy, our travelers spread out on the ground and turned in for the night. They fell asleep immediately, and master and dog competed with each other's snoring.

How long did they sleep? Who knows? But the stars still shined when Don Chipote gave the order to march. After stretching their torpid limbs, they resumed the trek.

Don Chipote and his dog spent many long days walking without a single moment of dismay. He was still inspired by the luring words of the deceiver Pitacio, and had not hesitated in abandoning his family; he had decided to brave all manner of hardship for the well-being of his loved ones. His dream was to go to the United States, which grew nearer as quickly as his legs would permit.

One month had passed in his painful pilgrimage. The traces of such an awful excursion could be seen on master and dog from a bird's eye view. Naturally, the provisions prepared by Doña Chipota had not taken into account such a long stretch; likewise, Don Chipote did not know how far the place was where he was going. So they finished the sack of *gordas,* then started to economize. And when the opportunity presented itself, Don Chipote bought a ton of tortillas and chili peppers. But since the tortillas were the first to go, there were days when the two ate nothing but chilis, the result of which was that when they had to dispose of their digested food, it was so painful that they even cried out loud.

Our voyagers had completed a month of wandering, as we were saying, when they first spied the spire of a church in Ciudad Juárez, which Don Chipote recognized thanks to what the other chatterboxes had told him. When Don Chipote was sure of being close to the border, he dropped to his knees and thanked his patron saint for the miracle granted him. He thought that all sacrifices made during his long journey were worth at least one plain *gorda* and two with cheese. As a reward for all his toil, don Chipote found himself at the doorway to a nation that, according to what Pitacio had told him, was paved in gold. This traveler, Don Chipote, who had crossed the parched desert and who saw the oasis from afar where he had to quench his thirst, quickened his pace, notwithstanding his weariness and the expanse of dunes that lay ahead before reaching Ciudad Juárez, which he believed would be his journey's end.

It would be six in the afternoon when Don Chipote and his faithful Skinenbones entered the narrow streets of the border town. No one took any notice of him. For as pitiful as his situation may have seemed, the inhabitants of that place were already accustomed to seeing this and even worse, because Ciudad Juárez is where caravans of *braceros* go to emigrate from their fatherland in search of work, obligated by the disgrace of our Mexico.

Don Chipote and his companion would walk for a long time, searching for a place to spend the night, but the poor guy did not have enough money to pay for a room, especially since most people were used to being paid in dollars and charged through the nose. And for that reason he was forced to spend the night on the railroad station platform.

He lay down on his floor mat, with his dog at his side. Touched by the tepid beauty of the night, Don Chipote began to think about his family and felt all that a father feels when far from his children. He sent them his blessings and went to sleep.

4

Ciudad Juárez, one of the largest border crossings in Mexico, is without a doubt one of the greatest centers of movement and one of the greatest centers of perversion as well. It is for this reason that the Americans, strangers to our country's interior, have formed such a negative image of us. It is there that drunkards from El Paso go, lusting for a drink to ease their craving, to escape the prohibitionist laws. Prostitution, so persecuted yet so sought after in El Paso, has its own district in Juárez. So then, if there are no real industries to be found there, there are the *cantinas,* casinos, and brothels. And this is the city in which Don Chipote spent the night, sprawled out sweetly on the planks of the railroad station platform. His dream had suddenly been granted to him, and he had no intention of waking up. Were it not for a well-placed kick in the pants by a Juárez cop, he would have certainly continued to dream about his little Chipote children.

But upon feeling the tender point of the policeman's boot, he jumped to his feet with a start, while Skinenbones snarled at the person who took such liberties with his master.

"Wassamadda wit ju? Jesus H. Christ, looks like you really got stiffed when you paid for this joint," said the despicable policeman.

Don Chipote did not understand the "wassamadda," but he thought that it was the complement to the kick. And not wanting for him to repeat the joke as he rolled up his little mattress, he told the officer, "Nothin', man, I was jus' leavin'."

"Alrighty then, but I want to see you moving along," replied the flatfoot as he continued to wake up the other peasantry in a similar manner.

Don Chipote did not stop to tie his knapsack before flying the coop, not only because he was afraid of the officer, but also because he was hungry. Since he hadn't eaten the night before, he was ready to eat a horse. His lucky stars led him to the market. And approaching a waitress, he asked her for a bowl of *menudo.* In no time flat, Don

Chipote and his dog were splitting a soup-bone. The waitress was shocked at the voraciousness with which the two pounced upon their food, but they took notice of nothing but the plate in front of them. When he finished his great feast, Don Chipote paid; and, asking the waitress to tell him where the bridge was to proceed to the other side, he got up, determined to set on his way to cross the great divide.

Unfamiliar with the formalities which one must perform to enter the United States, Don Chipote sneaked around the Mexican watch-post and went directly to the *gringo* border station; but, upon reaching the last building, one of the officers who patrolled the passage way spun him back around with a whirl. At the same time, Don Chipote's ears turned back to hear "wassamadda" and who knows what else, of which, we already know, he did not understand a single word.

Not satisfied with merely impeding Don Chipote's passage, the officer took note of Don Chipote's grimy appearance and directed him to the shower room in order to comply with the procedure that the American government had created expressly for all Mexicans crossing into their land.

Don Chipote could not understand why they treated him that way. And since he could not understand a thing they were saying, he stopped in his tracks. Believing that they would understand him, the poor guy said, "Hey, man, I ain't gonna do ya no harm. My name's Chipote de Jesús María Domínguez. I wanna go to the United States, I . . . I . . . I . . ."

Just as he was about to utter the next "I," he was forced into a room where his fellow countrymen were taking off their clothes to enter the shower.

When the *gringo* guard left, Don Chipote asked his compatriots why he had been taken there. Everyone laughed at his naiveté, but someone explained that it was necessary for him to bathe and disinfect his clothing before he could go to the other side.

Don Chipote did not wait another second. He thought that if this was the only thing he had to do, it was not worth fussing over. After taking off his clothes, he was naked as a jaybird, putting his grubby little paws in a box of powdered disinfectant, then hitting the showers. There thou hast it: Don Chipote actually taking pleasure in the first humiliation that the *gringo* forces on Mexican immigrants!

We will never know how Skinenbones was able to sniff out a way into the building, because, when they took his master away, they left him outside. However, such was the case that when Don Chipote least expected it, his faithful companion shared with him in the delight of a warm shower.

It was no small task for Don Chipote to scrub off all the grime that covered his body. An advocate of the saying that "the bark protects the tree," the washings that he had given himself were few and far between, and even those only came when a storm had fallen upon the fields. Be that as it may, however, he enjoyed having stripped off the husk he wore, and even more so when he figured that this was all he needed to do to cross into American territory.

When the delousing was over, he went to the room where people wait for their clothes, which, after being placed in fumigating steam, appear as neatly pressed as if they had just come from the tailor shop. After receiving his bundle of clothing, Don Chipote began to get dressed. But, thanks to his marvelous luck, those tatters had shrunken so much from the steam-cleaning that his clothes looked as if they were made for one of his little Chipotito children. Nevertheless, since he had nothing else to wear, he had to put them on and become the laughingstock of all those who saw him.

Don Chipote's humiliation did not stop with being the butt of all the jokes. A victim of circumstance, he endured the embarrassment and followed the others to the office where they prepared their immigration papers and had to pay the eight-dollar fee, something that Don Chipote did not know about. Our hero did not have the money to pay. He spent long hours of waiting his turn and was now at the point of becoming impatient for a few victuals, for he had not cast a single morsel of food into his bottomless pit since having thrown back that bowl of tripe in the morning. His stomach growled as if to say, "It's suppertime . . ."

When his turned arrived, Don Chipote sprang to his feet like a cat. But this is where all his difficulties began, because he did not understand anything that they told him. So one of the officers had to call in an interpreter; and, with his help, the agent learned that his name was Chipote de Jesús María Domínguez, that he did not know how to read or write, and that he had no money to pay his fee.

This being said, they made him aware that he could not cross because he had not fulfilled the requirements. And, showing him the door, they made him understand that he was in the way and should just shove off. This he did without delay, frightened that they might call the *gringo* cop, who would give him another round of wallopings.

The afternoon began to fall upon dog and master. With sadness painted upon their faces, they wandered through the streets of Ciudad Juárez.

Completely ignorant and unfamiliar with the surroundings, poor Don Chipote did not know who in God's name he could trust or where to direct his steps. Moreover, the few cents that he had left began to run short. But, urged on again by his voracious appetite, he headed to the marketplace. After having guzzled down a bowl of *menudo,* which he shared with Skinenbones, Don Chipote set out for the Central Plaza, where he spread out on one of the benches. Just about that time, a policeman was watching him very closely, because he was a stranger.

Moments later a mariachi band belted a march into the air. This was followed by the waltz *"Te volví a ver,"* which lullaby put Don Chipote to sleep, while Skinenbones went on full-alert to guard against any attack on his master.

When the serenade was over, the audience abandoned the plaza. And one solitary night-walker after another could be seen crossing towards Devil's Alley.

Don Chipote launched the clamorous notes of his snores into the air, as Skinenbones remained on constant vigil, guarding his owner's desolate shell.

The clock on the Customs Building showed eleven, then twelve midnight. And Don Chipote gave no signs of life other than—it is my unpleasant job to report—the vileness that he let escape through his mouth and, one after another, through his posterior duct.

Skinenbones began to become uneasy, and demonstrated this with his quiet whimpering. But Don Chipote continued his beauty sleep, for his gorging on tripe had satiated him so profoundly that he was certain to sleep there all night.

However, that's not what came to pass. Skinenbones could not contain himself any longer and let out a howl with all the force of his little doggy lungs.

Moments later, a policeman, alerted by the canine cry, woke Don Chipote up, More asleep than awake, he could not answer any questions to the satisfaction of the cop. After the cop gave Don Chipote a good whupping, he sent our poor hero marching to the slammer as his final destination. And as evidence of Chipote's infraction, he brought along Skinenbones to boot.

The distance between Ciudad Juárez's Central Plaza and the jail-house was not very great. And since the officer appeared to have been in a hurry to provide his guest with new lodging, he clubbed and beat Don Chipote all the way, making sure that Don Chipote did not rid himself of the daze acquired from the first big thumping. The cop did not miss a step providing Skinenbones with one swift kick in the rear after another.

With the haste the *gendarme* demonstrated, not five minutes of such a brash apprehension had gone by before accuser and accused stood in the presence of the police commissioner.

That civil servant asked Don Chipote the customary question, which goes something like this, "So what's the charge?"

The officer of the peace replied, "Public intoxication, loitering, and refusal to comply with the orders of a police officer."

Don Chipote, still feeling the bewilderment produced by the blow to his noggin given to him by the cop, realized the slander of which he was being accused and attempted to prove his innocence. But when they asked if he knew anyone to pay the fine for his misconduct, Don Chipote was not able to satisfy the police chief. Don Chipote had no other choice than to give up and spend the night awaiting his sentence. Since there is no one who does not have at least a touch of kindness in his heart, the commissioner allowed Skinenbones to accompany his owner to his cell.

The accommodations were not what we'd call very nice, and the company even less so. But Don Chipote had no other option than to accept it. So, looking for a little nook, he prepared himself to pass the rest of the night, while trying to ignore the stench given off by all the drunks.

After the cell door closed, Don Chipote realized that he was not going to spend the night alone, because there was a gang of drunks scattered all over the floor, their snores competing even while they slept off their inebriation.

Making himself as comfortable as possible, and with Skinenbones at his side, Don Chipote began to ponder what exactly had happened to him. He could not explain why they had treated him this way—he, who had never hurt a soul, who had never had a run-in with the law. For all of his conjecture, he could not figure out why things had turned out the way they did.

At four in the morning, the prison guard came to cut short his sad meditations as well as the winos' deep sleep. And following the custom of that time, he took the prisoners out to sweep the city streets. Once in formation, they were each handed a broom; and, accompanied by half a dozen cops, they marched off to pay for their sins. Once in the street, they began to toil.

Don Chipote, who had not believed what had happened to him even while sleeping, said to hell with his journey to the United States and began to understand the trick Pitacio had played on him. So while scratching at the earth with his broom, he thought it would be best to shove off for his *rancho* as soon as they let him go free.

The prisoners stopped working around eight and returned to the City Hotel to await their hearings and sentencing. But before they went in, as a special treat, the drunks were allowed to cure their hangovers in a fountain in order to ease their queasy stomachs. Then the guards made them clean the toilets, but not without having first deposited what they had eaten the previous day. And like "monkey see, monkey do," Skinenbones had no objection to voiding his guts of what he had already digested from the night before in the company of his master.

Don Chipote had to suffer a similar irreverence by way of Skinenbones. For while the dog attended to his gastric necessity, one of the policemen took notice of it and obligated his owner to sweep it up and wash the spot where lay the precise contents deposited by Skinenbones.

Don Chipote had no other choice than to comply with the badge and, while turning his face away, he lifted the offending mass.

The work now completed, the officers called the prisoners in an orderly fashion and they were lined up in front of a judge, because the time for trial had arrived. As a result, in less than the blink of an eye, they found themselves awaiting judgment.

Don Chipote shook with fear, while the others trembled from the hangovers they bore.

The first defendant stepped up, and, after the rigorous ceremonies, the judge sentenced him in this way: "Thirty days in the quarry. No fine."

The judge appeared as if he knew no other tune and sang the same ol' song to all the other bums. So when Don Chipote's turn came, he was ready to repeat the same tune; but, because Don Chipote was the last one in line, the judge stepped up to him, wanting to make a more detailed interrogation. That's why he made Don Chipote tell him his story from beginning to end.

When the judge finished listening to Don Chipote's yarn, he was convinced of the absurdity of the charge, and he promptly let Don Chipote go free.

Judgment now passed, that which they had taken from him the night before was returned to Don Chipote. Before justice could change its mind, master and dog made like a banana and split.

5

Don Chipote flew out of jail like a bat out of Hell; for a number of blocks, he didn't even look back, afraid that someone might be chasing him. But once he believed the coast was clear, he began to wonder about which path to take. Since all he had left was a single semolian, and because he was already taking a ride on the hungry-train, he had no other choice than to blow the last of his loot to quell his stomach's yearning.

After cramming down a bowl of *menudo,* which he split with Skinenbones, Don Chipote decided to look for work to make a little money, so that he could either go back to his *rancho* or cross to the other side . . .

He directed his steps to the train station. And he arrived with such good fortune that, in less than two shakes of a dog's tail, a fellow who had just arrived from Mexico's interior hired him to carry his rigging and valises.

Don Chipote, exhausted from the long night spent in jail, was barely able to do the job, and he wanted to just forget about it when his patron held open a hotel door. Don Chipote cursed the devil himself. But, upon seeing that they were almost there, he girded up all the strength in his spindly body and, with push after push, he made it up the stairs. After he completed said task and placed the bags in the indicated spot, he waited for his tip, which did not take long in coming. His benefactor took out a few coins, which dazzled Don Chipote, because the poor guy was not accustomed to making so much money all at once. For him to earn that much bread while working on the rancho, he would have to poke at an ox's ass from sun-up till sundown. So, with thousands of adulations to demonstrate his gratitude, Don Chipote took leave of his patron, lavishing upon him infinite praises.

Just as grateful as he was enchanted with the loot he had just made, Don Chipote went out running in search of another catch, which he did not take long to find. In those days, they were putting up barricades around the waterway of the Río Bravo to prevent the city from flooding. And that's where Don Chipote got a job.

He put in six days working on the rescue team, during which time he had made friends with his colleagues, who—knowing the reason for his journey and why the *gringos* had sent him back, and because he did not know how to read—entrusted themselves to give him the scoop on the tricks of the trade needed to cross the border in ways which did not satisfy the Immigration Act. One of them went even further. That afternoon, when they got off from work, he took Don Chipote to the home of someone who devoted himself to smuggling people across the line.

After introducing themselves, they explained the purpose of their visit. The *coyote* spelled out how he could help, saying that it was really a great deal, and that this was the easiest way for Don Chipote to get to the other side without running the slightest risk. He would charge him only ten dollars and would throw in Skinenbones for free. Thus the contract was sealed and an appointment was made for the following evening.

Don Chipote could not contain his glee, for it seemed to him that the moment would soon arrive when he'd find himself in the land where, according to what Pitacio had told him, the streets were paved in gold.

The next day at suppertime, Don Chipote asked how long he had stayed, and he paid the amount he owed for the nights he spent while still waiting to receive his paycheck. He was left with fifteen pesos.

It began to get dark when Don Chipote presented himself at the house of the *coyote* who was going to take him across. And there he was, amid a multitude of Chicanos, who, incapable of crossing the line in accordance with the law, had procured the services of that scoundrel.

When night fell, those little lambs, lead by the *coyote*, started out on the road to the outskirts of town with bearings set on the smelter in El Paso, Texas. Everyone kept utterly silent, following the *coyote's* instructions.

They walked for a long time in formation, and because they knew all the things that could go awry, they marched with their hearts beating out of their chests. Don Chipote, who had never had any reason to hide himself before, not only felt his heart beating, but also came to feel a wet spot forming in his pants, and he could not explain why this would happen without his consent.

Skinenbones sniffed around but did not bark—for they were so fearful of what might happen if he let out a howl that they had bound his snout with a bandanna.

At last, the *coyote* said halt and ordered them to wait as he approached the riverbank to get the lay of the land. It did not take him long to return. He instructed them to roll up their pants. Once completed, he told them to fork over the loot. And, in the blink of an eye, he nearly left his poor compatriots broke. But, as they knew, no one could say a word in protest.

So, with muffled steps, they neared the border and began to cross. Don Chipote was the first to go, because he thought it best to just go for broke. But the *coyote,* cognizant of the fact that one gambles with his life in these undertakings, was very careful to place himself at the back of the pack. Thanks to the good luck of those that were abandoning their fatherland, the electric company's whistle sounded nine o'clock when all had made it to American soil.

El Paso, the American city from which Mexican immigrants are able to see and pine for their native soil (which they have found themselves obligated to leave due to its own disgracefulness as well as the ambitions of our revolutionaries), is one of the corridors through which Mexico has lost most of its people. Don Chipote found himself in this city—where thousands of Mexican *braceros* come with the hope of putting an end to the anguish they have suffered back home— a city where so many proletarians have found protection against the persecution of the Mexico's ruling party—in the company of other countrymen expatriated in the shame of not being able to make a living in their own land—who, lured by the luster of the dollar, abandoned their own land to come to suffer even greater hardship.

Without having to agree upon it first, as soon as they were on this side, each one took whatever path appeared before him. And in no time at all, Don Chipote was seen with no other company than that of his faithful Skinenbones. He then directed his steps toward a hamlet the Mexican community had constructed around the foundry. And, as the distance was not far between the river and the electric car lines which make the rounds to downtown El Paso, he did not take much time getting there.

Because the majority of the inhabitants of the smelter were Mexican, it was very easy for Don Chipote to find out all he needed to know. So the first Chicano he bumped into gave him the lowdown on how to get to El Paso and let him in on where he could sleep that night.

Don Chipote did not wait any longer and went to the trolley-stop, which was close by. It did not take long for master and dog to climb onto that big cart which moved without oxen, and consequently made Don Chipote believe that it must be possessed by evil spirits. In his trepidation, he made the sign of the cross and prayed that the wagon would take him to wherever God wanted him to go.

Not much time had passed after he sat down on the rock-hard seats—where, in spite of his fear, he felt very cozy—when one of his partners who had crossed the river with him got comfortable next to Don Chipote. They recognized each other immediately. And as the trolley car started to move, they let their tongues fly and updated each other on their plans.

Don Chipote, who had not had anyone to chew the fat with since leaving home, took out all the contents of his knapsack for him. And the other guy, who was named Policarpo, returned the favor in kind.

The car's arrival in the Plaza de San Jacinto, or the Plaza of the Alligators, as the resident Chicanos from El Paso call it, was all they said it would be. As soon as they piled out of the trolley, they were forced to dodge charging automobiles to get to the sidewalk in front of the Sheldon Building. The tight spots in which the trinity, formed by Don Chipote, Policarpo and Skinenbones, found themselves in were not few, escaping from a cart with rubber wheels just before it made tortillas out of them. But, once they were out of harm's way, following the directions given to Don Chipote, they proceeded down an El Paso street in search of a place to spend the night.

The attention which this triad called to itself was not insignificant, for from afar one could see that they were *green*—which is what they call those who have newly arrived from the fields. Moreover, the poor guys walked slack-jawed, completely wowed and stupefied, looking at all that God had granted them. The *campesinos'* astonishment grew with each passing moment. They thought they must have been dreaming on seeing such elegant and lavish houses, for the best home they had ever seen was the *hacienda* owner's house, which looked like a shack in comparison to the edifices which were so tall that they appeared to be lurking over them. They marveled at the smooth streets, all of the people dressed so swell, and, more than anything, so many big carts that ran without mules; all these things simply could not fit into their imaginations and made them open their mouths to the point of drooling all over themselves.

It would be twelve midnight when our foreign friends, after having crossed San Francisco, San Antonio, and Overland Streets as well as all the numbered streets up to 6th, knocked on the door of a building that looked like a hotel, where they requested lodging.

The hotel's clientele (or whatever you want to call it), was all Mexican—men who had worked six months on the *traque* and were *en route* to their native homes carrying a few crumpled-up dollars which they had saved after a great deal of sacrifice.

Because of the prohibition and the restrictions on callgirls, that class of hotel was a haven for such vices. And without fail, it was never without two or three times as many women as male guests, in addition to the madam or hustler of the establishment. They would pick the pockets of the miserable wretches who, after working in the deserts where they put down railroad ties, did not hesitate to blow all their loot on cheap floozies, who one way or another would leave them with nothing to return to their homeland.

Don Chipote and Company had knocked on the door of one of those hotels asking for asylum. The night hostess did not wait long to show herself. And being a connoisseur of the trade, at a glance she realized that these would be easy cows to milk; therefore, with thousands of salutations, she bid them enter.

Don Chipote, who had not been the object of so much attention since he had left home, believed in his heart of hearts that this broad must have been his guardian angel. For, in spite of his shabby appearance, the hostess nearly fondled him.

Once inside, the madam showed them a giant book and told them that they had to sign their names and jot down where they had come from and where they were going. But because neither Don Chipote nor Policarpo knew how to form a single letter, she filled in the register with all courtesy and asked them to draw an X instead of signing their names. The requirements thus fulfilled, she invited them to follow her to their room. Once there, she turned on the light for them and, wishing them a good night, she took her leave, but not without first suggesting to them that if they needed anything, they should call her, and she'd come right away.

The room which she had assigned them was not the greatest. Nevertheless, she had discounted the price a dollar a head. The sum of all the furnishings consisted of a single bed, a cracked mirror, a chair, a pitcher of water, and, as a special bonus, an army of bedbugs that paced up and down the wall in hope of victims from whom to draw their daily sustenance. But the two journeymen, not satisfied with the little extras, decided to kill them. Once tired of the bedbug massacre, Don Chipote and Company untied their bundles, smoked fat cigarettes, and began to remove their clothing with the objective of turning in for the night. After all the day's commotions, their bodies demanded a little peace and quiet.

Like good Christians, they did not want to turn in without first praying a little something for the peace of their souls and to receive Heaven's blessings. So, as soon as they had formed a quorum, counting Skinenbones, they jumped to it, choking their rosaries and sending their blessings from one to the other. Then, without further ado, they went nighty-night.

Once they were in bed, more on the other side than on this one, they heard a knock on the door.

"Who is it?" asked Don Chipote.

"It's me, boys," replied a woman's voice. "Open up!"

Don Chipote, though poor, had the semblance of a good upbringing; thus, having been taught never to deny the request of a lady, he got out of bed and opened the door to see what she wanted. But the moment he opened the door a tiny bit, that lovely lady slipped inside without saying a word. Don Chipote was surprised, but not so much as not to reciprocate the hug the dame gave him. Once the skirt detached from Don Chipote, she took out a small carafe from her bosom and invited them to take a swig, for which Policarpo began to get up. Don Chipote was not the type to prevent anyone from partaking of the fruit of the vine, and because of his proper education which recommended never saying "no" to a lady, he toasted the betty before Policarpo was able to get out of bed. Neither Don Chipote nor Policarpo was a regular drinker. As a result, it only took them a few swigs to get tanked. They began singing, while the dame divided her affection between them in equal parts. Later, because the wine had risen to the tips of the hairs on Don Chipote's head, he asked Policarpo to whistle *El Abejeño,* and he invited the skirt to waltz. The proposition required no discussion, and Policarpo began to whistle the forgotten melody as the couple cut a rug.

When they had finished with the booze, Policarpo was no longer whistling, but instead was spitting pure saliva. Don Chipote, for his part, was dragging his feet instead of dancing, but he would not free himself of the betty's lure. All the while, she just waited for them to pass out, so she could do what they do to all the unsuspecting fellows who stay in that hotel every night.

The party carried on for a long while, and the dame had begun to worry about being able to get Don Chipote and Company tipsy, when suddenly Policarpo stopped whistling, or rather blowing spit, and let his body fall on the bed. Don Chipote, upon seeing this, probably went to get him up. But, he, too, was able only to fall into bed on top of Policarpo, where he also passed out cold. That dish, who had been waiting for just this to happen so she could have her way with them, let them fall sound asleep, then went through their pockets as a fish goes through water. She searched every nook and cranny, extracting from them all the dough they had. Then she left them to sleep off their drunkenness.

After the lady closed the door behind her, Skinenbones snuggled up to his master; and Don Chipote, thinking that it was the dame clinging to him, kissed the dog and then continued snoring. This is how Don Chipote spent the night, on into the following day, due to the effects of the little nightcap that he had tossed back. He was in the deepest sleep, all the while cuddled up to Skinenbones. As for Policarpo, he was not left behind, and played a duet with Don Chipote's snores. Only Skinenbones, who had never seen his master with his eyes closed after five in the morning, began to become uneasy.

It was more or less eleven o'clock in the morning when Policarpo gave Don Chipote a smack to the face when rolling over in bed. And, even though Don Chipote was sleeping full-bore, he was able to see stars and opened up his eyes. With his head still in the clouds, and hung over, he woke up Policarpo to ask him to explain his conduct. But, realizing Policarpo would just say that he didn't know what Don

Chipote was talking about, and that if something had happened, it was only a dream, Don Chipote let it go with a laugh. It did not last long, however, because his hangover, with all of its horrors, began to make its presence felt. And between the two princes, they filled the water pitcher that they had put out to be washed.

This being the first time that Don Chipote had ever gotten loaded, he did not understand what had caused his unquenchable thirst. So Policarpo explained to him what a hangover was, its effects and its origins, as well as the peculiarities of the cure, which, according to Policarpo, was to get a drink in order to finally get one's gullet going again. However, as all things must run their due course, they thought that the best thing to do was to leave the room and set sail in search of something to eat, so as to regain enough strength to go look for work. So they left the room.

Once in the street, the threesome began to look for a place to get a bowl of *menudo,* which, according to Policarpo's prescription, was the best thing for a hangover.

It did not take long to find what they call here a "restaurant." But, once they noticed the curtains arranged to block out the sun, they said it must be a whorehouse. Restaurant or brothel, that was where they were heading. And as soon as they snuck in, they took a seat.

Right off, a *gringo* ushered them in and asked for their order. But they did little more than stare at him, because neither of the two understood a thing he said. Luckily for our heroes, however, there were other Chicanos chowing down at the next table, and these other Chicanos were already versed in *tok inglis.* So, to get Don Chipote and Company out of their jam, the other Chicanos ordered for them.

In less than the blink of an eye, Don Chipote and Company were grubbing on a bowl of oatmeal, ham, a couple of eggs, and all that comes with a *gringo* breakfast. Both of them had eaten ham and eggs on such few occasions that they did not even know what to call the dish. They felt like the happiest men on earth, savoring the succulent breakfast. But despite all the vituals' scrumptiousness, Don Chipote got a lump in his throat just thinking that perhaps his little Chipotito children and his wife might not be able to meet their needs.

In the end, despite his misgivings, he attacked his food so quickly and closely that he almost forgot about Skinenbones, who, with moribund eyes, hoped for something to fall from the table. The neglect was soon rectified, for once Don Chipote realized that he had left Skinenbones out in the cold, he immediately provided the dog with his rations, which he had ogled so well, while Don Chipote and Policarpo puffed on a Prince Albert.

As you will recall, Don Chipote had made eighteen dollars on the job that he had done working for the rescue of Ciudad Juárez. You will also remember that of that sum he repaid the three semolians lent to him until he got paid, and ten dollars to the *coyote* and one for the hotel room. So he was left with a total of four clams. Unfortunately for him, you will also recall that the broad, who had given Chipote and Policarpo drinks and got them drunk the night before, had plucked them clean after they were tipsy. So, when the moment arrived to pay for their breakfast, they were at a loss and in the biggest pinch of their lives. The waiter did not want nor could he understand the excuses which Policarpo gave him. And he would have sent him to jail, if not for someone recommending to the owner that it would be better to make them pay for the food with work.

Said and done. After heaping grosses of curses upon them in English, he pushed them into the kitchen and made them wash dishes, which they very happily consented to do, afraid that the *gringo* would take legal action. Thus, without saying a peep, they grabbed the rags that they were given and started to pay with the sweat of their brows for what they had eaten.

6

As much as they hated having to wash dishes, Don Chipote and Policarpo could be nothing but grateful to the restaurant owners for giving them the opportunity to get out of the fix in which they found themselves. More than that, upon nearing completion of their task, the owners provided them with a plate of scraps, so they could have something to eat and would not go hungry until the following day. As for Skinenbones, he partied the whole day. In his little doggy recollection he could not remember having such an opulent day; while his owner was scrubbing dishes, he was gobbling down all the swill that they threw his way, through it cost him a few scratches from the cat, who realized some stranger was trying to swipe his food.

This episode, which had such a happy ending for Don Chipote and Company, was over when the owners of the restaurant felt our heroes had sufficiently paid for the food that they had gulped down that morning. Saying "gudby," so that Don Chipote and Company would take a hike, they showed them out the door. And, there you have them, shabby and bewildered, but in the United States.

Once in the street, with nothing to fill their pockets but their two hands, they thought about a way to go about looking for work. So they decided to stop the first person who passed by and ask him for information about where they might be able to find a job. Because he who asks shall receive, they quickly detained someone who, by the color of his skin, looked Mexican.

Policarpo, the more clever of the two, was the one who took the initiative and asked all the questions. "Scuse me, Mac. If ya'd be so kind. Can you tell us where we kin git a lil' work?"

Looking confused, the interrogated one replied in English, "What did you say? I don't speak Spanish."

Neither Policarpo nor Don Chipote understood anything that this guy was saying to them, but it never had occurred to them that he, who showed so clearly his origin, would not understand them. At any rate, completely disheartened, they continued on their way as the fellow who did not speak Spanish made fun of his poor compatriots.

I don't want to go any further without first providing a brief analysis of the weakness of some Mexicans who, like the guy approached by Policarpo, cross the border and forget how to speak their language. Disgracefully, these people abound. And they, who have come to the United States with one hand covering the holes in their seats and the other looking for a handout—who like the majority of Mexican immigrants have suffered immeasurable mistreatment by our *gringo* cousins, doled out to those of us who work on the railroad—have forgotten even the parish in which their fat heads were anointed when they were baptized. They speak a few words of English and boast of being *gringos,* especially when they come across fellows who are fresh off the boat, to whom they brag about their knowledge of *tok inglis.* These people, like all Mexicans who live in search of work, have received infinite humiliations at the hands of foremen and have even served as slaves to blacks, who, in order to keep the railroad companies happy and to maintain their employment, make our compatriots work like animals or worse.

However, these Mexicans become so conceited with the "fine" manners with which they are treated that not just a few have come to deny their fatherland without any more justification than that of having tried ham and eggs, which, it seems, makes them the worst thorn in the side of the Mexican *bracero,* who has come to this country in search of a piece of bread for his family.

Can there be any greater wickedness than that of these bastards who, passing themselves off as *gringos,* refuse to speak their own language, denying even the country in which they were born? I think not.

From these renegades—who are neither fish nor fowl, who speak neither Spanish nor English, who are, in a word, ignorant—is where the harshest epithets about us have come. So, then, all this talk about *cholos, greenhorns* and *dumb Mexicans* is reason for them to stick up their noses at the new arrivals from Mexico.

It was one of this class of disgraceful people that our heroes stopped to ask for information about where they could get work. And we have already seen the ridicule of which they were made victims.

Bereft, shall we say, they continued on their way deeply contemplating the idea of a dark-skinned *gringo.* But, since the question about where to locate a job remained, they decided to ask one more time. But this time it was Don Chipote who did it, because Policarpo had taken some offense at the dark-skinned *gringo's* teasing.

It was Don Chipote, then, who bumped into another fellow, who was one of those who, even though he had all the mannerisms of one who has lived in the United States for a long time, has only learned a mongrel form of English.

"Hey, boss," Don Chipote said, "look, we ain't got a single cent 'tween the two of us. Ya wouldn't happen ta know of anywheres that we might be able ta swing a job, now, would ya?"

"Ha! Get a load o' these fellas!" replied the man. "Looks like you two are green from head to toe and fresh off the turnip truck. Well, sure—over there are the recruiters who send out everyone who stops by for a job. Heck, it's workin' on the *traque*. But there ain't nothin' else here that they'll let a Chicano do. Look, o'er there's the agency askin' for folks to go to California. Jus' go up there. Only folks that don't want a job don't git one."

Policarpo, upon hearing that bit of information, removed the scowl from his face. He said to the guy, "Hey, buddy, would ya be so kind as ta do us the favor of takin' us to see if they'd find us a spot? You know this place awready. So we'd be much obliged if'n you could lend us a hand."

The fellow understood Don Chipote and Company's predicament, and, remembering the jams that he had gotten himself into when he had first arrived, he volunteered to take them to the office and arrange for their employment. And so, said and done, they crossed the street and went up to the office which recruited people to go to California.

As usual, a work contractor went straight to them, like a cat to a saucer of milk, purring at them the litany which they know in their sleep: "Come in, friend, we have assignments in all parts of the United States. Thirty-five cents an hour. It doesn't matter where you want to go: the Santa Fe or the Southern Pacific . . . They'll take you there and give you a return ticket after six months."

In the border cities, El Paso among them, their exists a certain class of people who are Mexican and who devote themselves to taking advantage of the innocence of our countrymen. Without any scruples whatsoever, they become instruments for the companies and landowners, who, knowing that Mexican *braceros* can be useful in all types of work, put Mexicans in those recruitment offices, drawing most of their employees from them, the majority of times, as frontmen or callers, who attend to shipping out greenhorns to the *traque* or to the cottonfields, where the workers are usually treated like animals. Those slavedrivers, who make their living from Mexican disgrace, appear to be our guardian angels when we come across them. Because the majority of us cross the border without a nickel and only dreams, and because those lobsters go out even to the middle of the street to offer us jobs, where they promise us not only a good salary and fair treatment, but even a trip back home to boot. Caramba, one can't help but believe that there are angels walking the Earth. And to receive their blessings, all the Chicanos dive in and tie themselves down, which is how they get all of us to carry a pickax and shovel.

This or something similar had to have happened to our chums after seeing that the work contractor, who without a doubt had a job order to fill, invited them with thousands of salutations to come in so that they could sign up. And with the dignified air of a skilled orator, he offered them some grub and a bunk.

It didn't take much spit to convince Don Chipote and Associates, because this was exactly what they were begging for. So, in less than two shakes of a dog's tail, they were jotted down for the first tour out of town, only they would have to wait until the entire order was filled.

"This's made it all worth while," said Don Chipote, giving thanks to the guy who had taken them. "At least, we hope so. The only thing that gits me is how're we gonna make it 'til we start workin', 'cause we don't have a thing ta eat."

"Don't worry," the other answered. "The Supply will give you food when taking you to the worksite and until you receive your first check. I don't wanna make it seem like they'll give it to you for free. No, siree, they'll give you the food on credit, then take it out of your wages."

"That's jus' fine with us, sir. 'Cause being how we are, we ain't got nothin' more than pitchers of water keepin' us filled," observed Policarpo. And, with that, the recruiter left, wishing them farewell.

Almost immediately afterward, the work contractor called for his contractees to go eat. Our chums, not knowing where their next meal would come from, had stuffed themselves with the leftovers they had been given at the restaurant and, now, did not have much of an appetite. Notwithstanding, since one shouldn't look a gift horse in the mouth, they went in to eat so as not to snub their tutelary angel.

The railroad companies and the Supply are in cahoots. And, like the recruitment offices, they are dependent upon the same system. Thus, once the *braceros* are assigned to a job, they are forced to buy from the Supply which, from that moment on, has a forced clientele, obligated to buy merchandise at their whimsical prices, with the one and only advantage of being able to charge the first payment. And this is why the work contractors give food to those they bring in, because they know that as soon as they begin to work, the Supply wrings every last penny from them to the point of leaving them with nothing but a bill when it's time to get paid.

Don Chipote and Policarpo had thought of only smelling the food, which consisted of soda crackers and cans of sardines and were already so old that they weren't any good except to stimulate the digestive juices and make their mouths water.

The only one who did not hold back but took advantage of his ration was Skinenbones. For, notwithstanding the tummy that he had put on in the restaurant, he stuffed himself on all that his masters threw away and that they would have to pay for later.

7

Three days had gone by since Don Chipote and Company had enlisted themselves to work on the *traque*. This was the same day that, according to them, they had begun to live like kings, because they slept as long as they wanted and the only thing that made them get out of bed was the fact that the sardines and crackers they had eaten the day before were now fully digested and insisted on leaving lickety-split. This is something which, as the reader knows, is extremely important to attend to or risk peritonitis.

Since they had nothing else to do than to eat and surrender to bodily pleasures, as soon as they felt the first gastronomic warnings, our immigrants didn't wait a moment to make their contributions to nature, unlike high society people, who are obliged to dissemble even in the most routine function.

For three days, then, they had slept, eaten, and sung their time away, when the labor contractors announced their departure for the following day. The contractors had decided to send those they still had in "the cage" to the sections where the foremen were short on beasts of burden to hammer down the railroad ties. That's why, once notified, they instructed the workers to pack their knapsacks and, if possible, to sleep with their clothes on, because the train left very early in the morning, and they needed to be there even earlier to check in their bags.

The caged birds received the news with some degree of satisfaction, for they were finally going to leave and start making a living for themselves, and to do this they had to actually start working. What Don Chipote didn't like was that as yet the work contractor had not said anything with regards to Skinenbones, but informed him that same day that he should look for a place to leave his little doggy, because the company did not provide passage for anyone except those going to work.

Don Chipote didn't say a word to the labor contractor, but he decided that he was going to either take his dog with him or resign from his job. As he would later tell Policarpo, he felt it wasn't fair for him to abandon Skinenbones, now that it looked like he had it made, just because the work contractor had said so, especially considering the fact that Skinenbones had been there with him right from the get-go, through thick and thin, and especially now that the ball was really starting to roll, beginning with this train ride.

Policarpo took Don Chipote's side, of course, and they both started to look for a way to take Skinenbones with them, even if they had to smuggle him on board. That night, after supper, everyone complied with the contractor's directive to make their bundles and pack their bags. And, while everyone was occupied, our buddies racked their brains to figure out a way to bring along Skinenbones. But all was in vain, for they couldn't figure out a way to fold the dog in half. But, more importantly, even if they did find a way to fit him in, how would they be able to make him stay quiet, particularly when he had to get rid of the food he had eaten? This was simply impossible. So, when the time came to hit the sack, they went to bed thinking that, if the directors refused to admit Skinenbones to the chorus line, Don Chipote and Company would stay the night and leave the dance in the morning.

They say that all things come in due time. And with that in mind, they stretched out their legs and began snoring, getting a late start due to all of their worrying and carrying on. On the other hand, Skinenbones, who was the cause of so much commotion, had been catching Z's for some time now, not giving a hoot or a holler about whether they'd take him or leave him behind.

The courthouse clock showed five in the morning. And, as if he were moved by the same spring, the labor contractor shouted to wake up his boys.

"Let's go, fellas! Rise and shine! It's time! It's time to get ready for the job and put an end to your vacation. Be sharp! The train leaves at seven!"

As soon as they saw him, the flock of Mexicans got to their feet and started running about. Of course, Don Chipote's troubles just got worse. But, since necessity is the mother of invention, he waited as everyone tied up their bundles, when a light bulb turned on in his head. He asked Policarpo to pack their bags but to leave out a *sarape* for him.

Don Chipote promptly took Skinenbones out to the street to give him the opportunity to dump out whatever he might have in reserve. The dog, who surely understood what all the fuss was about, did not like to be coerced, but did what he could. They went back to their quarters. In a corner, Don Chipote spread out the *sarape* which Policarpo had left for him. Still in it were all the cracker crumbs left over from what they had gobbled up. Once Skinenbones made his way into the middle of the *sarape* to start eating, Don Chipote wrapped him up in a bundle.

Skinenbones didn't cause any ruckus. He had never really enjoyed the honor of being carried in their arms, so he liked the arrangement very much and took advantage of it.

While Don Chipote did his packing, Policarpo readied everything else. So when the labor contractor gave the order to march, they were among the first to comply.

It's common for inhabitants of El Paso, at all times of the day, to see the pilgrimages of their compatriots as they, with packs slung over their shoulders, are led to the Union Train Station. For those of us who have been through those trying times, it is sad and painful to remember having been in the shoes of these transients, who, often ridiculed, are obligated by economic necessity to resort to labor contractors to find work so that they can send a little something to their families back in Mexico.

But let's put all these digressions to one side for a moment and continue following our countrymen, walking behind the contractor. They sauntered, almost blissfully, to who knows where, for the contractors were the only ones who knew where they were headed and had the responsibility of doling out laborers to the sections where they were needed.

The pilgrimage continued along the streets of El Paso until it reached San Francisco Street. The Mexicans marched up to the station and, making a turn at the ticket counter, were rounded up like sheep to wait until the labor contractor had made all of the arrangements for the trip.

When they finally came to a stop, Don Chipote thanked the heavens above, for, though Skinenbones didn't have much meat on his frame, he wasn't exactly made out of air either. As skinny as the dog might have been, carrying Skinenbones around like that was wearing on Don Chipote.

It didn't take long for the labor contractor to return. He told our compatriots to follow him, and he took them to the platform scale so that they could weigh their bags. This they did, one after another, and received claim tickets. Don Chipote's turn arrived. And though he was worried, he placed Skinenbones on the scale. Skinenbones, for his part, did not move a muscle, because his telepathy certainly made him aware of how Don Chipote was trembling for his safety. The operation went off without a hitch. But after they threw Skinenbones on top of the mountain of luggage to put into the baggage car, Don Chipote asked that they let him carry his bag onto the passenger car himself, telling them that he had a few things in his bundle of utmost importance and personal value. They permitted him to fetch his bag without any objections. Don Chipote didn't wait one second. So, with a knot still in his throat, he grabbed the bundle which was his beloved companion.

After the ticket agent finished weighing all of the workers' luggage, the labor contractor told the group that it was time to board the train. Our fellow countrymen boarded and made themselves comfortable in a car attached to the regular train. Their mouths gaped in amazement at seeing such an expensive room filled with such nice and soft chairs.

Once everyone had situated himself as best he could, the labor contractor brought out pots of beans, salmon, and sardines, as well as the indispensable saltine crackers, which they spread around for everyone to start digging in. Since it was now the designated time to attend to this chore, our compatriots dedicated themselves with tenderness and care to taking good account of the food advances which Papa Supply gives to his children, the workers, with love.

As soon as Skinenbones smelled the sardines and heard the gnashing of teeth, he got ready to eat and started licking his chops. But he was afraid, and rightly so, that this time he was going to end up like his friend, the butcher's dog, who stares at all of the meat but never gets any. All in all, Skinenbones didn't really believe that Don Chipote would forget about him; so, while no one was looking, he stuck out his head and his companions began to give him his vittles. Skinenbones started to jump up and down for alms because this was how he made his living.

The clanging of a bell and a jolt from the locomotive made everyone return to his seat. Don Chipote, who had never in his life been propelled by more force than that of his oxen when walking behind a plow, blurted out a Hail Mary, crossed himself, and began to pray the Act of Contrition for the peace of his soul. But because his companions were more keen than he, they began to make fun of him. So he got up his nerve. And, as the train's swaying began to soften, he calmed down and even put his head out of the window and watched as the train left behind a serpentine cloud of smoke, which disappeared in the distance.

Now, readers, here you have Don Chipote on his way to California.

Will he make it?

Those of you who have been hooked into working on the *traque,* tell me. Does he have much left to go?

With wheels turning and whistles whistling, the train carried this herd of our fellow countrymen, who, for one reason or another, had come to work in a foreign land—had come to expend all of their energy and perhaps even their life in this country, which in spite of being religious and supposedly democratic—that is to say, the land of the free—does not hesitate to kick Mexicans around. And so, as we were saying, with wheels turning and whistles whistling, the train set out to cross the arid deserts of New Mexico and Arizona.

After their departure from El Paso, they traveled all day on their way to Albuquerque, and by night time, they arrived at a station called the Isleta, which is located just before one comes into said city. Once at this station, all of the *braceros* got off the train. Like lambs, they were made to walk in single file right up to a big tent, where Papa Supply doled out something to warm his children's bellies. Looking like death warmed over and heated with just campfire flames, a pot of beans boiled next to a kettle of coffee, or something which looked similar. Our compatriots, almost numb from sitting for so long, were very happy to stretch their limbs for a moment. They were marched directly to the Supply tent.

Chicano comrades, for better or worse, very rarely lose their sense of humor. So, though tired and hungry because they had not had a bite to eat since that morning, they began to make jokes about the beans which, according to all probability, were going to be for them.

And what of Don Chipote and Policarpo? What had happened to them? Why were they not seen around there?

Quite simply, knowing human weakness and taking into account the troubles that Skinenbones would attract—he who had not revolted in spite of the discomfort of his trip—as soon as they saw the opportunity, they went out to the back of the big tent, untied the bundle and let the dog do whatever he wanted to do. As soon as Skinenbones was free, after waiting as long as he had waited just for an opportunity to be able to do his business, he did all he could, without blushing or caring about his owners' presence. This business could not have been small, if one takes into account the amount of crackers that he had eaten in the days it took to arrive. Good reader, have you ever had to burp so bad, and felt so satisfied when you finally managed to let it all out? So you can just imagine how good Skinenbones felt after evacuating enough digested crackers to fill a plaza. After Skinenbones finished his bowel movement, Don Chipote spread out the *sarape* once more and invited the dog to return to his hiding place; this Skinenbones did, though grudgingly and with a certain repugnance, for he had only two bowls to choose from: Be obedient or . . . get left behind.

Shortly thereafter, Don Chipote and Policarpo went to the soup kitchen in time for the labor contractor, spoon in hand, to serve bowls of beans and boxes of saltines to his pupils. And so, their ration received, his little boys began to gobble down the typical Mexican meal, which, as is often said, was like a blessing from God, because they were so hungry. True, the beans were not fully cooked, and could as well have been used as projectiles in the event of a fight. But because beggars can't be choosers, and any seeds are good for planting a fallow field, our heroes pounced upon the enemy with vigor. And without paying attention to good manners, in less than the blink of an eye, the kidney beans were in their stomachs. But our countrymen were still hungry. Fortunately, the kettle had plenty. And, at the invitation of the labor contractor, they doubled their ration. The servers began to pour a solution of *ocote* smoke or burned maize, which they claimed to be coffee, into a pewter tea cup that in broad daylight one would say hadn't been washed in years. But, be that as it may, our friends accepted it gratefully, for now full, they needed something to warm their chests. So, while burning themselves with the coffee, they took out tins of Prince Albert and Bull Durham, and, as a special treat, they lighted up with little puffs.

Naturally, with tummies full and happy of heart, even more so after topping it off with a smoke, the workers soon began to talk about their families and where they were from. They had already started to go very deeply into their lineage when the train whistle from the east made them jump to their feet and line up, because the labor contractor, at the same time as the whistle, gave the order to get ready; according to what he said, this was the train that they had to take to continue on to California.

The flock of sheep left the tent and waited in an orderly fashion for the convoy to come to a stop. This didn't take long, because the iron horse approached at full-steam. When its brakes squealed with bursts of air, the whole group let go like gangbusters, trampling one another to get the best seat.

Don Chipote and Company waited for the wave to pass. They were scared, and with good reason too, that in one of those free-for-alls, Skinenbones would start barking and botch everything.

Once all their buddies were on board and the way was made clear, our pals boarded the car. They found a seat right off, thanks to the fact that there were enough for everyone. They had scarcely made themselves comfortable when the locomotive's bell answered the conductor's "all aboard," and the convoy lunged into motion.

The train quickly picked up speed. With a full head of steam, it began to quickly traverse the dry regions of the state of New Mexico. Our compatriots, pleased and put to ease by the succulent dinner and the rest they were enjoying in their seats, cut loose the joy which follows the Mexican people everywhere they go. And because it never fails that someone starts singing, the strumming of strings was soon heard. After the guitarist up front played some chords, he announced, "Awrighty, now! Who wants ta give 'er a whirl?"

Since there were no *señoritas* around to impress, the majority responded, "Yeah, let's give 'er a go."

As it was impossible for the musician to play back-up for everyone at the same time, he decided that they would take turns, two by two, so that they could sing in tandem. And with a "do-si-do and away you go," the first duet started it off with the following:

If you only knewww
How much I love youuu
My tiny one
You're the love of my liiife
And could be my spoiled wiiife
My tiny one
If you just, if you juuust
Give your love to meee

They repeated the former one more time, as was customary, then followed with the most sentimental verse.

I don't want love untruuue
All I do is dream of youuu
My tiny one
C'mon, come onnnn
Give your love to meee

When the singers finished, the excitement was overflowing. And there were cheers and applause for them. Then, with the permission of the assembly, the next pair took their place and let loose the following:

When the mockingbird commmmes
Comes to sing, my love
Let it sing, my love
Let it sing
Let it sing, my looove
Let it siiing

It's three in the morniiing
And you don't come, my love
What wouldn't I give

to be close to youuu?
And you don't come, my looove
Come to see meee

And it's three in the morning, and it's three in the morning, and . . . because they didn't know any more, or because they just forgot, they stopped to hear the clapping and the congratulations that were expected. And since we are all romantics by nature, and the song had awakened the memory of past loves, the singers and listeners were very pleased to hear another chorus.

The jubilee grew. And to these songs they kept adding others and others, making more people willing to do their howling interpretation of songs from the native land.

When everyone in the company had warmly performed their services for the audience by singing, and there was no one left to perform but Don Chipote and Policarpo, they took it as their invitation. And they, having caught the fever of their comrades' glee, accepted the invitation for their silvery voices to ring out. So, without a big to-do, like people of little pretense, they took their places, coughed, and cleared their throats. After agreeing upon the song they were going to sing, they let fly to the air the following:

Gentlemen, I will sing to you
About all the animals I have seen
I've seen four raggedy pigeons
Weaving calabash trees
Out of a piece of fabric
Showing me all their teeth
Which were so bright and shiny
That they looked like ivory
Counting more than two thousand
And one gigantic fang
But the one thing I ain't never seen
Is a parrot that could breast-feed
Yes, I've come across some amazing things
But I ain't never seen a parrot breast-feed
I've seen yellow parakeets
Who growled at the coyotes

And a depressed cockroach
Boiling up sweet potatoes
I've eyed a bumblebee
Yoking two wild boars
And there was a toad with spats
Who traveled on horseback
But the one thing I ain't never seen
Is a parrot that could breast-feed
Yes, indeed, I've seen some incredible things
But I ain't never seen a parrot breast-feed
I've seen a rooster fight
A bull with a little red brow
And a little cricket
Drinking wine at the bar
I've eyed a team with a cat
And a gator, tied together
And a pheasant shooting
A lamb with a shotgun
Blowing his head to smithereens
Blowing his head to smithereens
But the one thing I ain't never seen
Is a parrot that could breast-feed
Yes, I've come across some amazing, incredible, marvelous things
But I ain't never, ever, I said, I ain't never seen a parrot breast-feed

The acclaim received by Don Chipote and Policarpo could be compared only with that given to the author of the great play *Sangre Yanqui*. Of course, when they turned to the crowd, all demanded that the pair to grace them one more time with their wonderful voices.

Don Chipote and Policarpo were about to repeat that lovely composition, when Skinenbones, who had heard his master's much maligned notes, could not resist the urge and added to the air a note from his own chest, which put all the comrades, and particularly the labor contractor, into motion.

They immediately began to look for the person who had belted out such a mournful lament, because, due to the precautions Don Chipote had taken, the last thing they thought was that Skinenbones would be accompanying them on their pilgrimage.

Don Chipote and Policarpo did nothing more than look around and cross their fingers, fearing that at any moment their faithful friend would be discovered, which happened shortly thereafter. Skinenbones, surely annoyed by going *incognito* all this time and wanting to be counted among the party, launched a second discordant note into the air, which helped the searchers locate the origin of the lament. They headed straight for the bundle.

Taking it away, untying it, and putting Skinenbones in plain view was done in the blink of an eye. There was general surprise among everyone. And, as expected, the labor contractor began to let loose with Hell's Dictionary, which didn't bother the dog one bit. Wagging his tail, he went up to Don Chipote and started asking to be petted.

Don Chipote didn't even see or understand the trouble his faithful dog had gotten him into. But the labor contractor, turned wild man, came up with the solution to the situation very quickly. He decided to swing Skinenbones by the tail and throw him out through the window. And he would have done it too, were it not for the *braceros*, who protested *en masse* and told him that if he did such a thing, he would be going down the same road. The beloved labor contractor had no other choice than to bow down before the sympathy which the dog had inspired among the Chicanos. So, swallowing his pride, he put on a happy face, gave the dog a few scratches, and said that it had been just a joke, thus reprieving Don Chipote's illustrious companion.

8

It was eight in the evening when the train stopped to drop off the first shipment of Mexicans destined for the *traque*. Since the labor contractor had never forgiven Skinenbones, he decided to get rid of the dog the first chance he got. So, calling to Don Chipote and Company, and two more of the doggy defenders, he told them to grab their things and go, for they had now reached the section where they would stay. And with no time to lose, they promptly readied themselves, saying good-bye to their travel companions with just a glance and stepping off the train. The locomotive lunged into motion at once. And, in no time at all, its shape was lost in the distance, while Don Chipote and his pals remained with their mouths agape, wondering where to go next.

Since the section foreman had already been informed of the shipment, as soon as he saw from his house the train's arrival, he directed his steps to the little depot to pick up the new pupils. After spotting them, he introduced himself by way of hand signals, in English, and in the few words of Spanish he knew. He quickly made them understand that he was the boss and that they should follow him to their quarters.

They didn't make him tell them twice. They followed the boss in a single file.

The headquarters was practically right in front of them. So they were quickly assigned to rooms, two in each, and the foreman went on his way.

Other compatriots already at that depot went to pay a visit to their new companions right away and filled them in about all they would have to do. They also brought them dinner and tinder to make a fire.

While the Chipote trinity guzzled down what the visitors had brought them, their compatriots asked them about Mexico—if it had righted itself yet, and all the questions that one would ask of those other just arrived from the fatherland.

Our protagonists answered with the little that they knew, trying to be neighborly to those who had received them so kindly. They jawed for a long time. And around ten o'clock, their visitors took their leave, recommending that with the provisions they had left for them they make their "lonches" to take to work in the morning, because the "old man," as they called the foreman, didn't like anyone staying behind and not working.

Our friends found a way to light the stove at once and warmed all the leftovers to make their "lonch," or vittles.

While Policarpo was cooking the beans in a pot, Don Chipote washed his hands and went to knead flour to make tortillas. Since he had never tried to bake anything in his life, he was soon covered up to his eyebrows in wheat flour, and the dough looked like oatmeal.

Policarpo came to his rescue. Between the two of them, and with more flour, they were able to knead the dough sufficiently to make tortillas. But they were trying to make them as if they were corn tortillas, in other words, patting them in their palms. As this procedure did not yield the desired results, they proceeded to make them like *buñuelos* and had greater success. A little imagination helps in these cases; so they concentrated. Using a bottle, they ended up making some *gordas* shaped like *huaraches*. And after cooking them, they discovered that they were edible, and the shape did not matter to them in the least. And so they continued to work.

While they were doing this, Don Chipote, who hadn't forgotten about his Doña Chipota and his little Chipotitos, in spite of many vicissitudes, remembered them even more with all the cooking. He imagined himself surrounded by his kids and Doña Chipota, on her knees in front of the grindstone, throwing out hot tortillas, while he made salty *chucos* for the little ones, as he ate everything that came out. Burning himself when placing a tortilla on the stove snatched him away from his reverie. He returned to reality and continued to prepare for his debut on the *traque*, or the "little gold mine."

The burn made Don Chipote keep a better eye out. And to finish the rest of the *gordas* he sharpened his five senses while the beans frolicked in the pot and began to turn red, a sign that it wouldn't be long before they were ready to eat.

For those men who have never stirred a pot in Mexico before coming to the United States, the culinary crisis is their first tribulation, for while working on the *traque* each man has to prepare his own meals or go hungry. Since there is no greater wax than that which burns, and since the stomach knows no etiquette, there's no solution other than to fix one's own chow. But since back in Mexico most of us are attended to by our old ladies just because we're men, here in the desert, where we don't have anyone to do these things for us, the first thing we do is cry—because of all the smoke.

Something similar happened to Don Chipote, for, although he was a farmer, in his home he was used to merely walking around the *comal.* However, as necessity has no shame, he was now fulfilling his responsibilities, for better or worse.

Some time had already passed after making their *huaraches,* or (according to them) tortillas, and all they waited for were the beans. Policarpo, giving them a good once-over, reckoned that it was about time to hit the hay. And so, without further ado, they cleared the floor, spread out whatever they brought for sleeping and turned in for the night, joining Skinenbones, who had been snoring like an angel from the moment they arrived.

Up late and exhausted from the long walk, they slept like a couple of logs for the remainder of the night. And they would have kept right on sleeping, were it not for the boss pounding on the door and telling them to go to work. Because the poor guys didn't wake up after the first few knocks, the foreman, with all courtesy, redoubled his hollering, accompanied with "hels" and "godamits," which got our countrymen out of bed, thinking that the house was falling down. Once they realized what was going on, they got themselves together quickly, packing some bean tacos and showing up ready to start work on the *traque.*

Meanwhile, their fellow workers were already in the *puchicarros,* or pushcart house, fetching their tools. So when Don Chipote and Company finally arrived, all the newcomers helped to do was to put the handcar on the railroad tracks.

The old man broke loose with some insults, but because everything he said was in English, it rolled off them like water off a duck's back. And since our partners were new and green, they had no other option than to weather the storm.

When everything was ready—the pushcart on the tracks, the pickaxes, crowbars, the shovels, "yacks," "rinches," in short, all that is necessary—the old man gave the order to ship out and everyone took his place. Don Chipote and Policarpo got stuck manning the cross-bar that is pumped up and down to make the car go.

Our chums had been cold when they woke up, but with all the exercise of pushing up and down, they soon began to sweat and stick out their tongues, giving it all they had. The handcar rolled along while the old man kept an eye out on the track, looking for a spot to get his workers to pick up or change the *tallas,* or railroad ties. He finally gave the order to halt. They took down their tools, removed the car from the tracks and waited for the old man to get up off the ground, because he carefully examined the rails while lying on his belly. He got up at last, commanding his people to ready themselves and splitting them up into groups, some with the "yacks," others ready to dig out the beams, and others to take up the old ties and insert new ones in their place. Both Don Chipote and Policarpo were assigned to dig; so, with pick-axes in hand, they started to toil.

They had given only a few swings of their axes when they spied Skinenbones in the distance, growing closer to them, running at full speed and with his tongue out. The poor dog had run after them, but soon got left behind. Nevertheless, he had chased after his master, certain of catching up to him, and he had not been mistaken; just a few moments after they had spotted him, he was at Don Chipote's side, dancing around and wagging his tail.

Don Chipote gave him a pat and went back to swinging his pick-ax. As soon as Skinenbones saw the water barrel, he took off to drink to his little heart's content until he had cooled down, because the long run had made him thirsty.

Skinenbones was licking his snout over and over again, when the foreman, who had spotted him, gave him a swift kick right to the gut, then asked who the dog belonged to. When Don Chipote made himself known, the foreman told him, with oaths and curses, to go to the depot to bring back more water to pay for the crime committed by his faithful companion.

As the reader will recall, this was not the first time that Don Chipote was made to pay for one of Skinenbones' deeds. So he returned to the section at a swift pace to refill the water barrel and get back to his work.

On the way, he thought about how long it had been since he had last seen his family. He prayed for the chance to tell them what had happened to him since he left. And even though he trusted Pitacio, he knew that nobody could take care of his little Chipotitos like he could. At any rate, he was intent on getting in touch with them. But how could he when if he didn't know how to read or write? He would have to search for someone among his fellow workers who could do him the favor. The most important thing was not to let more time go by without contacting his family.

Our hero reached the depot, brooding about sending a letter. He filled the water barrel and, after catching his breath and wiping away the sweat, he started back out again.

Tired from carrying the water barrel on his back, Don Chipote came to the place where his companions worked. The foreman, feeling sorry for him, gave him a pick-ax on which to lean, not realizing that the poor guy was ready to throw in the towel after hauling the water barrel for more than a mile.

This kind of treatment for the poor guys who work in the camps and in the railroad sections is so common that one doesn't even take notice. Moreover, on these jobs, the foreman is the slavedriver of the Mexican infidel, who has to do his bidding. He cares very little about the suffering of those who are so grateful to the company that employs them.

The author of this novel, not too long ago, had to join up with the infamous *traque,* like the majority of those who come from Mexico, and he took perfect account of the abuses which foremen commit against the workers. On one occasion, the foreman, for no other reason than because he could, forced the author and two other Mexicans to replace a "sweech," or direction changer, one half-hour before a passenger train was to come through. Take into account that one had to cut the beams and lift up the rigging, or the main part of those "sweeches," from under the embankment. Those familiar with this kind of work know perfectly well that this is impossible to do in half an hour, even more so with only three men. In spite of all of this, that foreman worked us like dogs, only making us desperate. The train arrived without our completing the task, and we had to fix it on the spot so that it could go through.

After this, the foreman began to yell at us in a manner so vile that, unable to take any more of his insults, I talked back to him. He socked me. And I returned his lick. I got canned, losing even the time I had already worked. Incidents like these happen daily on the *traque,* and not few are the foremen who have gone as far as killing Mexicans, such crimes going unpunished, just as there have been Mexicans who have sent a foremen to meet his maker. Of course, when the workers on the *traque* decide to rub out a foreman, it's because he's already heaped their plate high with injustice.

That breed of foreman had befallen our hero. And one can see what a swell fellow he was in considering the treatment that he had given Don Chipote when coming back dog-tired.

Don Chipote, who wasn't one to take abuse or to dish it out, but who also knew that he had left Mexico to work, took his tool and kept on stabbing at the ground.

The day went by without further incident. At four-thirty in the afternoon, the foreman gave the order to stop, telling them to put their tools on the pushcart and beat it for the station. After the drumming that the foreman had given them, everyone tried to duck out of working the cross-bar up and down, and as a result, they all stayed clear, one way or another, of that little spot. But Don Chipote and Policarpo, the greenest of the bunch, went straight for the hand-lever, for they thought it was still their turn. And without saying a word, they grabbed the handle and began to give it a little elbow grease.

Hoping to arrive quickly and jump into bed made them give all that they had left after their hard day's work. So they got home very swiftly for a pushcart. They all took part in putting the little cart back into its house, they stowed the tools, and they left, flying to their respective hovels in search of the rest that they so desperately needed.

Don Chipote and Policarpo had worked so hard that they didn't even feel like making supper. For a good long while, they just lay on their backs without saying a word, not having energy to do even that. Don Chipote turned over in his mind the opulence which Pitacio had told him about, saying that here people relished in thinking about how to serve him, but, from the moment he left his home, he had done nothing but suffer.

Anyhow, there was no solution for the predicament he had fallen into for the moment. And knowing the saying "Don't cry over spilt milk," he came to the conclusion that the best thing to do was to get up and make dinner and his lunch for the following day. Policarpo helped him right away, because, like he said, he could eat a horse.

In less time than it takes to tell, Don Chipote had washed his hands, rolled up his shirtsleeves, and started into his baking class. Naturally, this time, with the previous day's practice, he was more on the mark with his magical concoction. And the ball of dough was soon ready for flattening under the rolling pin (or the bottle, which was all they had supplied him).

While Don Chipote was preparing the aforementioned dough, Policarpo washed the beans and readied the pot. But when he went to light the stove, he discovered that they didn't have any firewood chopped.

Since he had no other choice than to chop firewood, but not wanting to swing a hatchet, Policarpo convinced Don Chipote to do it, telling him that, he would dust and sweep up the room and make their beds or whatever they had for sleeping.

Don Chipote, who was not the type of person to complain, went out into the yard, picked up the ax and, more from necessity than from desire, began to chop away at a beam. As soon as he had enough for the night's consumption, he stopped working, or better said, he threw down the hatchet. And taking an arm-load, he went to go start a fire in the stove, for he, too, was hungry enough to eat a horse.

The stove began to smoke right away and the dishes turned red hot. His pal Policarpo placed the pot on the stove, and it didn't take long to start making *gorditas*. Meanwhile, Don Chipote, bottle in hand, was giving it his all, rolling the balls of dough, while Skinenbones watched, mournful that not one scrap had fallen to the floor. Don Chipote licked his fingers every time he got burned. Finally, when the last *gorda* passed from the stove to the pile, Don Chipote felt sorry for Skinenbones and offered him something with all courtesy, assuming he would surely reject it. But the dog, with all courtesy, far from what his master foolishly believed, let go with such enthusiasm that, if he wasn't careful, he would have bit the hand feeding him.

Don Chipote was admiring his faithful dog's appetite when Policarpo called for his attention, telling him that their provisions were all used up and, according to what the foreman had explained to them, he had to make out an order to send it on its way to Needles, where the supply store was located. Don Chipote decided that, after supper, they would go to see one of their fellow workers so that he could write out the order for them, and ask him at the same time to please write a letter to send off to his family.

Policarpo agreed. And as he could no longer endure his hunger, he went to taste the beans. But to his dismay, they were still hard as rocks.

After such a disappointment, Don Chipote didn't wait any longer. And, giving another *gorda* to Skinenbones, he began to make salt tacos and stuff his face with them just as quickly as Policarpo, who, fearful of not getting his share, aided in the destruction of the mountain of stewed *gordas*.

The force with which those brave soldiers assaulted their enemy was so fierce that very soon not a single trace of the foe remained. And our heroes, feeling more than satisfied inside, felt courageous enough to destroy another enemy, who was as big or even bigger.

Since neither one was in the mood to cook, just to eat, they decided to fill up with water. And that's what they did, sitting down at once to recuperate from such a succulent feast.

Stuffing their faces had made them lethargic. They were already starting to fall asleep when Don Chipote remembered that they had no more supplies and needed to look for someone to make out their order. With the fear of going another day without food, Policarpo got up, and those two hapless souls, who didn't know even how to sign their own names, went to look for somebody to do them the favor of writing a few words to request their rations.

As luck would have it, the first fellow countryman that they saw did them the favor right away. And he told them that he was at their service whenever they might need it.

Don Chipote was delighted by the compatriot's kindness, so he asked him to write the letter to his family, which his counterpart was happy to do. And taking a pencil and paper, he waited for them to dictate the supply order to him.

Don Chipote and Policarpo just stared, because they didn't even know what to order, until their compatriot started to ask them questions.

"You want flour?"

"Yessir, if you don't mind," replied Don Chipote.

"What else?" asked the scribe.

"Well, hmmm, what else do you think would be good, mister?"

asked Policarpo.

"Do you have any beans?" he asked in return.

"Yessir, but they're the last ones. An' we awready put 'em in the pot. We even added a dash of salt. But since were awready so hungry, well, we ate the tortillas all by themselves."

Their comrade was no genius, but he couldn't stop laughing at these fellows' naiveté. "Awrighty then, I'll jus' jot down a few beans fer you guys."

"Gee, well, if'n you want to. If'n you don't mind doin' us the favor," said Don Chipote and Policarpo at the same time.

"What else, fellas?" added the writer.

"What else would be good?" the two guys asked him.

"You folks like ta smoke?" the one with the list asked them.

"You betchya," they replied.

"Okay, I'll put ya down fer some tobacca, an' meches, an' papers. What else?"

"Well, the truth is, sir," explained Don Chipote, "we don't know nothin' 'bout what folks eat 'round here. An' if'n they send it to us . . . Aw, shucks, if'n you'd be so kind, jus' put down whatever you'd git."

Don Chipote's bright idea was supported by Policarpo. And so their fellow countryman, making use of all his willing faculties, put everything he thought that they would need on the list. Once their order was complete, he read it off, item by item, while Don Chipote and Company recognized and praised the intelligence of the scribe for having hit the nail on the head with all the things that they wanted.

After the reading was over, our chums couldn't find a way to express their gratitude. As for their compatriot, he confined himself to telling them to take the list to the foreman so that he could send it off that same night, to see if it was possible for their supplies to arrive the next day.

Don Chipote commissioned Policarpo for the job, as he wished to stay behind to ask his comrade to write a letter to his unforgettable Doña Chipota.

As Policarpo left to complete his task, Don Chipote twisted and turned his hands, because he couldn't figure out how to ask his literate friend to do this other favor for him. In the end, since he didn't want to miss this opportunity, he said, "Say, mister, seein' how good you're wit' all this writin' stuff, do ya mind doin' me the favor of writin' a letter to send back home?"

"Be my pleasure," replied the other. "You jus' tell me what it is that you want me ta scribble down fer you."

"Okie-dokie. I'm much obliged."

His fellow countryman opened a paper notebook. He sharpened the point of the pencil on the ground, and he waited for Don Chipote's dictation, which was the following:

"My beloved Doña Chipota."

"Wait jus' a second," interrupted the maestro of the pencil. "Jus' let me put the headin' on." So saying and writing it were one as he put this down: "Peach Spring, Arizona, November 3, 1924."

"My sweet Doña Chipota."

Having written this, he asked Don Chipote, "Okay. Now what else?"

"My dearest Doña Chipota," repeated Don Chipote.

"I aweady got that," the pencil guy replied.

"That's awright," said Don Chipote, "this way she'll see how much I'm thinkin' 'bout her."

His fellow countryman did as Don Chipote pleased and continued to scrawl away, as Don Chipote kept on dictating like a chatterbox.

I wish I was this piece a paper, so I could see you and my little Chipotitos. But since I don't got two pennies to rub together, I'm sending you this, praying to Our Lady of Fermented Spirits that y'all are well. For myself, I'm in good health, thank the Lord. I wanted to let you know that I'm now working at a job called the *traque* which goes fixing the rails that the train passes over. If you could just see how sharp those *gringos* are! Because there are some things out here that even make Skinenbones gawk with his mouth wide open.

Here, the work administrator, that's not what he's called, he's called "boss," and when he's not around we call him the "old man," but he's so keen that, wow! me and a friend that runs around with me, named Policarpo, we've gotten along very well with the old man. And, guess what, he trusted us so much that he put us in charge of steering of a little contraption called a "puchcar." And no one else can touch it or make it go, except for us, so you see how highly he thinks of us.

Since he can't pronounce my name, he calls me "Chipoto," and he calls Policarpo "Polocarpo." But this is just every once in a while, because from the time we go to the work till the time we get off, he calls us by a very funny nickname that I don't understand too well. I think it's something like "Godam Sonovagun." I reckon he calls us that because he can't say our names.

If you can find someone to write a letter for you, send me one telling me how you have been, how are the crops, and how are my beloved little Chipotitos, who I want to see so badly.

Tell me if Pitacio is helping you. And tell him that nothing he told me I would find in the United States is true. All the good stuff is all used up already, and all I've come across are pure headaches since I got here.

Don't you forget to put the scarecrow out in the chili pepper field, so the birds don't eat the seeds. Sell the big hog, if you're ever needing something, but let the sow alone to see if she has more piglets come next year.

I won't write more because I reckon that the gentleman who is writing is already getting sleepy. Farewell. And pray to the Saint of Little Distilled Spirits that things go well for me so that I'll see you all soon.

Your husband,
Chipote de Jesús María Domínguez

Send your letter to Peach Spring, Section 7.

Don Chipote felt as if the weight of the world had been lifted from his shoulders, walking back to his room and holding the finished letter that he had wanted so badly for his family. Grateful, Don Chipote went back, as much to thank the swell guy who had done so much for him as to see if he could get two cents for the postage stamp from him, because he didn't even have a hole to fall dead in.

The good Samaritan, who understood what was going on, didn't make him beg very much and came through with the dough, which earned him the greatest appreciation from poor Don Chipote, who called him his guardian angel with all due respect.

They were thus engaged when Policarpo returned to the scene after turning in the order to the foreman. He said that the foreman had told him that he would send their order off as soon as the train passed through.

As it was already late, they said good-night to their benefactor and flitted off to go to sleep, but not without Don Chipote's first dropping off the letter at the little station house.

9

They were out like a light that night. And with good reason, too, for the punishment that they had endured on the previous day had been no trifle.

The sun was already high in the sky and the other workers were ready to leave when the foreman gave the order to depart. But upon realizing that two workhands were missing, he furiously stormed off to their room.

Don Chipote was dreaming about his little Chipotitos when the foreman started to knock down the door with his fists, making our two partners jump out of bed with a start. Weathering the storm that the foreman unleashed upon them, they went to the pushcart, leaving the old man to say whatever he wanted, because, in the end, they didn't understand a word.

The day went by like all the others, because there is no difference in this kind of work from one day to the next. It's always the same: Shovel, then pick, or, Pick, then shovel; one day here, the next day over there; but always bent over and suffering the foreman's abuse. There is only one day they get excited and that's payday. That's when they demonstrate their sadness or joy, for if not completely satisfied, at least they have enough spirit to continue to endure the foreman's inclemency. But this enthusiasm at receiving their paycheck usually ends up in rage, because, obligated to purchase their fortnight's provisions from the Supply, he who is granted the authority by the railroad company takes out whatever he wants from each of their paychecks; and the result is that the poor workers, for all that they try to economize, always come away with the short end of the stick.

One can hardly believe that the authorities of the United States have not recognized the robbery which victimizes our compatriots, for it is impossible that such abuses can pass undetected by them. In this case, the only thing one can assume is that: either they don't care because the victims are Mexicans, or they themselves are accomplices to the companies' shameless acts.

In the whole time that this writer had to work on the *traque,* he doesn't remember ever having received a paycheck consistent with the amount of time worked; nor had they ever received his rations as he ordered them, because the infamous Supply sends whatever it feels like and charges whatever it wants.

But one has no other choice than to suffer all of these injustices, for if one complains—that is if one can even do so, because not knowing the language, all you can do is swear, and this only in Spanish, which goes in one ear and out the other, he just gets more of the same.

Despite all the abuses of our fellow countrymen who come to work in the United States, there is not one who returns to Mexico and goes home and tells the truth. Everyone just comes home telling fishing stories and spinning yarns to the wives who ask them how it went for them in the Land of Plenty. This is why the majority of us who pass through these parts have allowed ourselves to come—as they say, to strike it rich. And, as we have said, it was due to the tales that Pitacio told Don Chipote that he abandoned Doña Chipota and his little Chipotitos.

Be that as it may, Don Chipote was now in over his head and had no other recourse than to put his nose to the grindstone at work. And that's exactly what the poor guy did, hoping to return to his homeland as soon as possible.

After returning from work on one of the many days that he spent tying down railroad tracks, Don Chipote found out that he had received a letter from back home, making him go plumb out of his skull with glee, because he was sure that it was from his Chipote family.

Choked up with emotion, Don Chipote looked for the fellow, who, according to him, was the most learned and well-read person in the world. And as soon as he found him, Don Chipote begged him to read him the letter he had just received.

His partner was glad to do him the favor. As they tore open the envelope, Don Chipote's heart was leaping out of his chest in his eagerness to hear about his family. The man of letters began to read, at last, relating to him the following:

Tepislatitlán, November 28, 1924

My dear companion for life, Don Chipote de Jesús María
Domínguez:

I reckoned that you must've already forgotten all about us, when
just this morning your pal, Severiano, came by and dropped off the
letter you sent me from that town with such a funny name. I wanted
to know what you wrote right that second, but, as you know, I only
got as far as grammar school and that was just to clean up the little
ones between the legs. So I had to keep my pants on until Pitacio
came in from the fields.

Once Pitacio showed up and I found out everything that happened to you, I could have just bawled my eyes out. But then I got
cross, because I recollected how you didn't pay no never-mind to
what I told you, and you just listened to what Pitacio had to say.

But now that that's over, I just pray to Saint Vincent that you'll
be back with us again real soon. At least now you know how to drive
that little contraption you say you drive for the foreman. And, when
you get back, you can look for a job in the *pueblo* to see if we can go
and live over there.

Pitacio has behaved like this . . . half good, half bad. Because,
if you're talking about work, he's more or less lazy. But, when inside
the house, he doesn't stop going back and forth to help me. And,
guess what else, he's already put in a pump for me in the kitchen so
I don't have to go so far for water. And that's not all neither. Because
he pumps it for me and won't let me pump it myself, he says, so I
don't wear myself out. So, with all this, you can just see how much
he really cares about you, because he does as much as he can for me.
But what I don't like is that he doesn't look after the farming,
because he wants to spend the whole day inside the house. So the
cornfield didn't turn up too much, because he didn't give it the second weeding.

As for the chili, yes, indeedy, he's sure taken care of that,
because that's what he likes best. Just the other day, I went to the field
ready for sowing, and he showed it to me, and, my word, was it ever
hot. And I tell you that just the other day, when he brung over his
chili, and we ate, it burned me so much I was even panting . . .

Wait just a second. Little Crispín just did something and the flies
are chasing after him. I'll just clean him up and get back to telling
you more. I'm done. And I'll just say, you know how you told me, if
I needed anything, to sell the hog and not the sow so that she can

have more piglets, well, I need lots of things. I don't think it's a good idea to sell the hog, because the sow can't make piglets all by herself. Because as you know since the cock died, the chickens haven't had any chicks.

In the end, I reckon you know what's best to do. So, in the next letter you send me, tell me if I should finally sell the hog, because the little ones have gone without any drawers and my only wool shirt is worn so thin that I can't figure out how to mend it.

Before I forget, I want to tell you that the priest has dropped by a few times asking for you. And then we shut ourselves in to pray so that things'll go well for you, and, above all, so that you don't become a Protestant. Because the father says that over there they convince people to give up the religion of their forefathers. So don't you let nobody talk you into becoming a Protestant. And if you do, you better just not come back, because the priest says that you'll burn in Hell.

Don't forget to tell me how Skinenbones is doing, and if he's still with you. But, most important, as soon as you have a little money, send me what you can so we can save the hog from the chopping block.

Uncle Calistro, the father of one-eyed Nicomedes, is doing this letter for me, because I didn't want Pitacio to do it, so I can tell you everything. Write back to me soon so I know how things are going for you. And, with this, I'll just tell you that the little ones say hi and I do the same, while praying to all the saints and martyrs that they protect you from all evil, and that you receive the blessings of your Doña Chipota who loves you very much.

Doña Chipota de la Encarnación Morada de Domínguez

His literate pal kept his trap shut, as Don Chipote remained ecstatic, with stars in his eyes and his mouth wide open, because the letter had transported him to the fatherland, where his Chipote family lived.

After a few moments, no longer hearing the good fellow's voice, he asked, "Is that it?"

His interlocutor replied, "Yep, that's all that's written here in the letter."

Don Chipote was not very pleased with the letter, because it contained a few things that he had not fully understood. But, frankly, he couldn't find a way to ask his chum to read it to him again so that he could better acquaint himself with all that Doña Chipota had said. The thing that concerned him most was when she told him that Pitacio didn't want to go out of the house; and, because he was pumping his wife, he didn't attend to the field when ready for planting. And if that wasn't enough, what about all this business of the father locking himself up with her to pray that things went well for him? He made the sign of the cross and wondered: Why didn't the priest ever feel like paying a visit when *he* was there? With such thoughts filling his head, it no longer mattered to Don Chipote that the sow wouldn't have piglets if she sold the hog, or that Pitacio had the field growing full of chili peppers, or that the cornfield went without the second weeding.

Poor Don Chipote! He loved his Doña Chipota very much and he trusted her so very much too, but with what she herself told him in the letter, he was becoming jealous of Pitacio and even of the priest, as holy as he might be.

In the end, he decided to ask his friend to read the letter one more time to him, and his pal very happily agreed.

Don Chipote got ready and, now all ears, listened carefully to the innocent yarns that his old lady sent to be read to him.

When the fellow who was master of the written word came to the end, Don Chipote had his head in his hands and was sobbing. His good buddy asked him why he was crying. And when Don Chipote explained why, his friend made him see that he had no reason to suspect his Doña Chipota, because the best test that he could give her was that she mailed him a letter telling him everything, not hiding anything from him. Because he could be sure that if she thought about doing anything, she would be very careful to keep it under wraps, so that her husband wouldn't find out about it.

After what his pal said, Don Chipote was almost convinced that his better half had not thought for one moment about pulling one over on him. But all this didn't take away the desire to grab a hold of Pitacio or that priest and give them a devil of a beating.

As we have already seen, Don Chipote was jealous. And as sure as he was of his Doña Chipota, he knew well that there would be gossip in the plaza that she had fallen into enemy hands. And he could be sure that, whenever he strolled by the plaza, he would never hear the end of it.

He decided then, in his heart of hearts, that when he completed his six months' contract and they gave him his return ticket, he would beat it for his home sweet home and would never cut himself from his wife's apron strings again.

They say ask and you shall receive. And as we shall see, what Don Chipote had planned came out backwards, for fate would have it another way.

After Don Chipote thanked the one who rescued him from his literary quandary, he went to his room, where Policarpo was fulfilling his culinary responsibilities.

When Don Chipote went inside, he already had set the big box, which served as a table, with a mound of *gordas* and the jug, which served as a pot, with a few dozen beans that spun clockwise from the last stirring. Policarpo invited Don Chipote to sit down, now that he had just finished kneading the dough and it wasn't worth it for Don Chipote to get his hands dirty.

Don Chipote, absorbed in thought over the conjugal dilemmas which burdened him, said that he had no appetite and that he preferred to go lie down.

Policarpo didn't buy that for one moment and asked him if the letter had contained bad news. Don Chipote replied, No, the only thing that they told him was to come back soon and to send them some money, because they were going through some hard times.

"That jus' gets my craw. 'Cause you've awready seen how that Supply store fetches back most o' these paychecks they've been givin' us. Seems like we don't work fer nothin' 'cept the food we eat. Now, let's jus' see if'n I'm left over wit' a lil' somethin' from this next paycheck that's comin' so I kin send it back ta them. An' I'm gonna tell that fella makin' out our food orders not ta put so many things on the list, see if'n this way I kin save me jus' a lil' bit more."

With this, Don Chipote cleared the floor. He made the sign of the cross and he spread out to rest after a long day's work.

Policarpo implored him two or three times to come and eat, because he shouldn't go to bed on an empty stomach, that he would lack the sustenance necessary to have enough strength for the following day's work. But Don Chipote, on his back, didn't pay him any attention and just tried to get some sleep to rid himself of the thoughts of his family which plagued him so.

Policarpo did what he could with the mountain of *gordas* he had made. And once he was full and his gut ready to burst, he rolled himself a cigarette. He washed the dishes, while giving little puffs to his cigarette, and prepared the grub for the following day. Then, making the sign of the cross, he cleared his little spot on the floor, just like Don Chipote, and sprawled out to saw a few logs.

There is no way for us to spend a peaceful night after getting such unpleasant things stuck in our heads, especially if it's a familial issue. Don Chipote didn't hear the bell toll one or two, because there was no clock in the depot. But, on the other hand, he did hear Policarpo's snores all night. His partner slept without a care in the world, expelling more air from up top and down below—that is to say, through his nostrils and his mouth—than a bomb.

Don Chipote turned to one side, then the other. He didn't like this position and turned on his back, then flat on his face. But, whichever way he turned, he couldn't keep his eyes together longer enough to catch any Z's.

He spent the night in agony, perpetually thinking that Pitacio, or the holy father, was giving his woman the time. But, when he was most sure of this, he remembered the words of his pal who had told him, "If she did somethin' wrong an' wanted ta hide it from you, she wouldn't be so candid as ta write ta tell you about it."

Naturally, this calmed down poor Don Chipote a little and almost made him sleepy. Although he was unable to find complete peace of mind, in one of these drowsy spells, Don Chipote overslept. The birds sang. The sun rose. The workers got up and went to the pushcart house. And our chums were still dead to the world.

The foreman, who didn't like for his workers to stay home, went to go roust them out again with all the anger that he was able to muster in such cases.

Our pals, who had now become accustomed to waking up on time for work, felt very cross that he would roust them out before it was time, according to them. So they were even about to start a row with the old man, not realizing that he had them between a rock and a hard place.

When they realized that things were not as they had imagined, they got ready in a jiffy. And chewing on a couple of tortilla tacos, they left to put their shoulders to the wheel.

Someone other than Don Chipote would have woken up in a frightful mood, not wanting to work and who knows what else, but good old Don Chipote—for he truly is good—went to work to do the best job he could in spite of the bad night he had spent. However, though his will may have been strong, he was extremely tired, and this made him start nodding off in spurts.

During one of these sleepy spells, no doubt the one where he slept most, the foreman got upset and went over to him and boxed Don Chipote's ear with a "godamit." Don Chipote looked all over himself as if a snake had bit him. Then he raised the pick-ax over his head as high as he could, And he struck at the rail with such bad aim, that, instead of hitting the beam, the pick-ax buried itself into his foot.

The wound he gave himself woke him up even more, but just enough to make him sit down and examine his foot, which was bleeding horribly.

As soon as they realized what had happened, the foreman and all of the other workers gathered around Don Chipote, trying to do something for him. One got out his bandanna and tied it around Don Chipote's ankle. Another ran and brought back the water barrel and started to clean the wound. Policarpo, the most concerned of all, ripped his shirt into shreds to make a swathe and bandage him up. And Skinenbones, who never left them, howled with grief at his owner's side, as if he understood how much Don Chipote was suffering.

Don Chipote made a big show of this pride that we Mexicans have, for as much as it hurt him, he said that it was nothing and it would soon pass. As happens in these cases, Don Chipote was the object of all the workers' attention, and even that of the foreman, who was generally a two-faced crumb like all the rest of them. He hastened to instruct the workers to place the pushcart on the rails to take the wounded man to station headquarters.

All of this was done in less than two shakes of a cat's whiskers. And, right away, Don Chipote, supported by one of the workers, was laid on top of the pushcart and sent speeding off to the depot, flying as fast as the human crowbars could move the cart.

Don Chipote suffered terribly. And with nothing to ease the pain, he was forced to take it, like a big boy.

Even at the headquarters—which is composed of nothing more than the pushcart house, the foreman's house and the workers' quarters—it's impossible to treat those who are victims of some work acci- dent. In such cases, the only thing that one can do is send them on the first train headed for the nearest railroad hospital. And so they attend- ed to Don Chipote the best that they could in his room, waiting for the first train to pass by to take him to a hospital.

The foreman ordered one of the men to stay with the injured party. Being his companion, Policarpo happily agreed, for he was so loyal to Don Chipote that he was determined to stay, even if they didn't tell him to. The others went back to work.

Don Chipote soon succumbed to shock and became delirious, see- ing in his lunacy the priest and Pitacio, his Doña Chipota and his little Chipotitos. And he thus brought Policarpo up to date on his problems.

That's the way it went for most of the day, alarming Policarpo to such a degree that he believed that his best buddy would meet his maker. Intent on seeing him through, Policarpo decided not to leave him even if he had to quit his job to do so. Thinking and doing were one and the same as he bundled up his shambles and those of his part- ner. He got everything ready and waited for them to return from work to ask the foreman for his time card and set out to wherever they took Don Chipote.

The workers arrived at the regularly scheduled time and they went right away to check up on the injured man, so Policarpo gave them the scoop. The old man showed up a little later. He informed himself of Don Chipote's condition and told Policarpo that the train which would take him arrived at ten o'clock.

Policarpo, who was as much involved as Don Chipote, gathered up his nerve and, without much beating around the bush, told the fore- man, "Looky here, sir, so's my friend doesn't go alone, I've made up my mind ta go with him. So gimme my time card right this second."

The foreman remained unmoved, because he understood Spanish about as well as Policarpo understood English.

Desperate because the foreman didn't understand, Policarpo tried to explain by way of hand signals. And praying that God would make him understand, he repeated what he wanted, using gestures and man- nerisms.

The old man realized what Policarpo meant, but didn't want to understand, because it wasn't convenient for a worker to leave him. But, as Policarpo insisted, he sent for the worker who spoke the most

English, not so much because he didn't know what this was all about, but so that he could explain things better to Policarpo.

With the interpreter before him, Policarpo screamed and stomped his feet to convince the old man. Having no other choice and unable to force Policarpo to stay on, the boss made out his time card so that Policarpo would get paid in Los Angeles, where the Santa Fe Railroad has a hospital for its workers, and where Don Chipote was being sent.

Satisfied that he was finally going to leave with what he had coming to him, Policarpo started to fix enough "lonch," or provisions, for the trip, because his comrades told him that Los Angeles was very far away.

After eating supper and making enough grub to cross the Sahara, Policarpo started to prepare a pot of wheat *atole* to give to Don Chipote for dinner and to bring as leftovers to give to him on the way. At once, he gathered the little bit of food that remained and divvied it up among the workers who had treated them so swell.

Not much time remained before the train's scheduled arrival when Policarpo was at last ready to give Don Chipote a bowl of *atole*, which he refused to eat, asking for water instead.

Moments later, the foreman showed up with the tickets. Now ready, Policarpo quickly bid farewell to the other workers and then, with the help of his comrades, carried Don Chipote to the station. Once inside, they repeated their farewells. The train whistled. It approached. It stopped. They put Don Chipote aboard. Policarpo boarded. The Iron Horse whistled again. And our fellow countrymen began their journey to Los Angeles.

10

Our buddies traveled full speed ahead without saying a word, because, in his pain, Don Chipote didn't feel like talking, and Policarpo kept quiet as not to disturb him.

The train into which they had been packed was the famous "Limited," or the Flier, as our compatriots called it. As soon as they got on, two seats were vacated, as much because no one wanted to sit next to the Chicanos as to accommodate for the injured party. And so, after acclimating themselves to their surroundings, Policarpo and Don Chipote stretched out their legs, feeling the satisfaction of sitting on something soft after having sat on the ground for so long. Likewise, since they had slept on a solid dirt mattress from the moment that they had arrived at the depot, covering themselves with only their *sombreros*, sitting in those chairs made them feel like kings, and the warmth of such a well-heated cabin filled them with ecstasy.

With all the wonderful accommodations, it did not take long for little bubbles of saliva to form and for a few puffs to be set free from down below. Quite simply, one could say that they slept like a couple of logs.

During the day, this would have been reason enough for the *gringos* who sat in the same car to complain and throw out our countrymen. But this happened without their knowledge, because most of them did the same thing while sleeping, so no one took notice of our pals' bellies, which played like a pair of accordions.

This is how our chums passed the night, and when they opened their eyes, they were already at Needles Station, the first city in California where the train stops.

After wiping away the sleep from his eyes and cleaning up the drivel that had been oozing from his mouth while asleep, Policarpo turned to check up on Don Chipote and see how he had spent the night. Don Chipote was still asleep and snoring profoundly. Since Policarpo was hungry, he immediately got out the knapsack where he had placed their grub, and he began to sink his teeth into the bean tacos with a heartier appetite than if he had worked all night.

After a few moments of moving his trap, Don Chipote woke up and Policarpo immediately asked him how he felt and how he had slept, to which his interlocutor replied, "I tell ya, I don't feel half as bad as I did last night. Maybe 'cause I was sleepin' like a baby."

With all diligence, Policarpo asked him if he was hungry. Don Chipote replied that he really wasn't, but Policarpo told him that it was necessary for him to eat a little something; if he didn't, he would be too weak to hold up against the treatments that they had to give him. And without waiting for Don Chipote to give his consent, Policarpo unpacked the pot of *atole*. He went out to the platform of the vestibule and started to warm it up with his matches. He was doing this when the train conductor came up to him and told him that it was not permitted. And even though he spoke to Policarpo in English, Policarpo understood. Using hand-signals, Policarpo told him that it was for a sick person who was going to the company hospital. The conductor then took him by the hand and dragged him over to the food car, ordering the Negro cook to heat up the *atole* for Policarpo and to give him some of the leftovers as well.

Policarpo was delighted by the conductor's kindness, but he was even more grateful when the Negro gave him a plate with a slab of beef, some slices of bread smothered with butter, and a cup of coffee, which Policarpo thought that the wounded party would gladly eat as soon as he saw it.

Policarpo went tasting Don Chipote's meal as he carried it down the aisle. So, when he arrived, he had to clean his whiskers.

Don Chipote really wasn't in the mood to eat right then. But upon seeing such a delectable hodge-podge, he let loose like a pig at the slop they had thrown to him, though not without first inviting Policarpo to enjoy this gift in his company.

Policarpo, who would have begged for alms, did not make him ask a second time. And with the whites of their teeth showing, they pounced upon the dishes.

Nothing was heard but the thundering of jaws engaged in this chore for a good long while. And, without even saying it, they competed to see which could gobble down the most food and not leave anything for the other. As a result, they both ate very well.

In such hurry, the banquet was soon vanquished. And after one lapped up the coffee and the other licked the plate clean, Policarpo went to the water fountain. After turning the faucet, he began to wash the dishes, which the *gringos* complained about immediately. The conductor came onto the scene and told him to take the dishes to the Negro so that they could be washed over there.

Policarpo returned to the kitchen on wheels and once more put into play his system of gestures to tell the Negro to give him some water to wash the dishes, which he happily agreed to do. The Negro gave him a rag to put on like an apron, showed him where the water was and left Policarpo to wash his dishes.

Policarpo started his kitchen detail and finished the job with much diligence. When the *gringo* conductor gave him the high-sign, Policarpo took off the apron, and was already on his way out, when the Negro told him to have another taco and to come back at meal time, so he could give him something else for him and his companion.

Since one shouldn't look a gift horse in the mouth, Policarpo jumped at the chance and promised that he would be ready by meal time to pick up their contribution.

Policarpo returned to Don Chipote's side at once and found him sleeping to digest his food. He was able to confirm this by the puffs Don Chipote was throwing out, accompanied by an occasional moan; as Don Chipote hadn't received any medical treatment other than the cleaning of his wound with water, which they had done at the depot, his foot was becoming more and more swollen, and it was as red as a tomato.

Policarpo felt sorry for his comrade, and careful not to jostle him, he laid down next to Don Chipote. Then, he rolled himself a cigarette and started to take little drags to dispel the monotony of the journey.

Meanwhile, the locomotive continued to belch smoke and pull the convoy over the iron parallels.

With his eyes half closed, Policarpo saw the stations, the *pueblos,* the cities all go by. In the rail sections, he saw other Mexicans bent over, pick-axes in hand, working like dogs, only glancing up to watch as the train passed them by.

In the cities and towns, he also saw the faces of dark-skinned women, who even waved to him. The train stopped in some parts; in others, it continued full steam ahead, without paying any attention to the hullabaloo made by the Mexican children, who screamed at the top of their lungs, greeting the passage of the iron snake that spanned the continent with dizzying speed.

It was two in the afternoon when the train entered the Santa Fe Railroad Station in Los Angeles. The brakes of the convoy screeched to a halt. The engine's bell kept ringing, as if to greet the populous Pearl of the West.

Policarpo, who had fallen asleep, woke up to the hustle and bustle of the passengers getting off the train. Startled by all the commotion, he rubbed his eyes and then nudged Don Chipote carefully, so that he would wake up.

Don Chipote, after peeling open his eyes, asked Policarpo, "Is we there yet?"

To which Policarpo replied, "Yessirree, my brother, we're in Los Angeles now. You git yerself ready fer me ta help ya git down whilst I fetch the bags."

Don Chipote attempted to stand up. But when he tried, a little moan escaped him. It would have been a scream if he hadn't bitten his tongue.

Don Chipote hadn't really suffered much during the trip, because his leg had lain across the seat. But when he tried to stand up, the blood shot down to his foot with such force that there was nothing else he could do but, letting out a groan, sit right back down again.

Meanwhile, Policarpo had taken down their luggage. And, after leaving it on one of the benches outside, he went back to help his friend get off the train.

When Policarpo got back to Don Chipote, he found him huffing and puffing like a bellows from the pain. But, since he had no other choice than to evacuate the car, he gathered his strength, and with one foot almost dangling, he descended from the car, or better said, was practically carried by Policarpo, while raising more Cain than if they had cut off his head.

Burdened with woes and moving at a turtle's pace, they were able to reach the bench where Policarpo had left their valises. They sat down. And taking from their bags all that our Lord had provided for them to eat, they started to look around from side to side, not knowing what to do or where to go.

The Santa Fe Hospital, where they treat all of the sick and wounded who work for the company, is situated in front of Hollenbeck Park. It has a little Ford truck to pick up those who come from the *traque* and can't get to the hospital under their own power. Drivers are always advised ahead of time about the train which carries sick workers, so that they can be at the station to pick them up. This time, like every time, they had gone to pick up Don Chipote. But, since Don Chipote and Company had gotten off on the wrong side of the train, they were not to be found. In the meantime, our pals, trying to kill time, as they say, rolled cigarettes and exhaled mouthfuls of smoke.

The hospital employees didn't take long to find our chums. So not much time had passed when they stopped in front of our heroes. After asking them a few rigorous questions to find out if they were really the guys that they were looking for, they told them to pack their bags and to go to the "trok" that was waiting to take them to the hospital.

Our buddies guessed at, rather than understood, what they had been told. And, since all Don Chipote wanted to do was lie down and be healed, he didn't play dumb. So he went to the "trok," supported by those who had come for him, as Policarpo followed with the bags.

Once in the back of the truck, our comrades were transported to another world, and nearly fainted—because this was the first time that they had ridden in a carriage that moved without oxen to pull it. After the shock of the first impression had passed, they just tried not to move, fearful that the animal would suddenly buck and throw them to the ground.

They still had distrust painted on their faces, their eyes opened wide and their hearts beating out of their chests, when the little Ford entered into the garden in front of the hospital. The driver stopped at the front door and told our pals that they had arrived.

Policarpo was the first one to set his foot on solid ground to take down the luggage and help his partner. But he didn't have time to do it, for, as soon as he opened his eyes, the employees had already transported Don Chipote inside like a soul snatched by the devil.

Don Chipote was taken to the office right away to register as an injured company worker. Like all of us who go to these lands, our fellow compatriots' jaws dropped to the floor in amazement, as they saw wonder upon wonder. With everything that was happening to them, they thought that they had to be dreaming.

Don Chipote had to give his vital information once more—that is to say, tell them who his father and mother were, where he was born, and everything else one needs to fill out the form by which one comes clean in confession before becoming one of the patients.

Once Don Chipote had spilled his guts of all that related to his person, one of the nurses pointed his nose in the direction of the room assigned to him, which made the poor guy extremely happy, for the pains in his foot were becoming unbearable.

Policarpo stood waiting in the office door with blood-shot eyes. As soon as he saw them cart off his buddy to another part of the hospital, he grabbed the suitcases and followed after him. But this time, they told him to stop. Showing him the door, they made him understand that the hospital was *not* for the well or the healthy. Don Chipote would stay there, but Policarpo would have to scram to wherever he thought best.

The explanation fell like a bomb upon our heroes, for, as our readers will recall, they had sworn not to split up, especially not in case of illness. But, as they had no other choice in the matter than to separate, they gave each other a farewell embrace, with their eyes watering and their hearts almost breaking.

The nurse comforted them, telling them it was no big deal, because they could see each other every day from three to four in the afternoon, which was the patients' visiting hour.

With this consolation—and because there is no greater wax than the one that burns—Policarpo dropped Don Chipote's bag. After giving him one last pitiful look, he left the hospital, worried about leaving his pal alone and shoving off to who knows where, for he had no more in his pocket than a tin of tobacco, a book of rolling papers, some "meches," or matches, and the slip of paper to get paid for his time worked. So, with only these bare necessities, Policarpo's predicament is understandable to the reader.

Finding his nerve, as those of us who have been around those parts like to say, and without a care in the world, he crossed the street and went into a park, where, seeing the grass so green, he thought about lying down for a little while to think about what he had to do. After looking for the spot that he liked best, he fell onto the two cheeks of his rear end, letting out one of those deep sighs that comes from that very profundity. He rolled himself a cigarette to puff on while he pondered what he was going to do. He was savoring the first drags of his cigarette when Skinenbones ran up to him from behind and started to lick him on the neck, while he whimpered as if complaining that they were trying to give him the slip. With all the difficulties of getting off the train, our pals had even forgotten all about their own dog. But because Skinenbones had his tail between his legs, he had stuck to them like glue, until those from the hospital had arrived and taken them away. Then he did, indeed, get left behind. But he chased after them at full pace without becoming discouraged. Naturally, notwithstanding all of the dust, he kept after them, aided by his snout. And you can now see that his strength did not fail him, as he had at last found Policarpo.

Skinenbone's arrival cheered Policarpo up a little, for with a companion like Skinenbones he didn't feel so alone in the world. Though it was true that Skinenbones couldn't help Policarpo, except to keep him company, misery does love company, as they say in those parts. So, for a long time, they were affectionate and congratulated each other for having found each other once more. Then, Skinenbones spread out lengthwise, not giving a straw about Policarpo's problems.

In the meantime, the sun had begun to disappear, and with the shadows that came, Policarpo started to see if there were some good place to spend the night—that is, if Fortune didn't have something else in store for him.

When he finished smoking his cigarette, he felt rested and his guts began to scream, "Chow's on!" Policarpo got to his feet and went more or less along the route that he had already traveled, because he wanted to remember it so he could return to visit his good buddy, Don Chipote de Jesús María Domínguez.

Because of all the running he had done to catch up to Policarpo, Skinenbones wanted to do nothing but sleep. However, since he had no way to protest, and with no other option than to hustle after him or get left behind, Skinenbones opted to follow behind Policarpo.

Carrying his knapsack, Policarpo went down Fourth Street and soon found himself on Santa Fe Avenue. Continuing down that street, he quickly made it to the train station. But instead of going inside, he kept on going until he reached First Street. Like a magnet, Policarpo approached the Placita without thinking, which, to tell you the truth, wasn't too bad for him, because he began to notice that many Chicanos were attracted to that area.

The sun had come full circle and shipped out for some shut-eye when Policarpo and Skinenbones reached the infamous Main Street, after having experienced a thousand and one frights at the hands of those darned automobiles, which tried to run them over every other second. Skinenbones didn't know to which saint he should commend his soul, for he was almost flattened like a tortilla by the autos a number of times. In this frightened state, the two reached First Street and, again, drawn like magnets, continued toward the Placita.

For those who have lived in Los Angeles for some time, it's nothing out of the ordinary to come across fellow countrymen, who, like our pal, show their greenness from a mile away. And, naturally, even though it shouldn't be the case, there is no one who doesn't stop to take notice of them. Being recent arrivals, they feel snake-bit and confused, having to ask about even the most insignificant things. Our countrymen's naiveté causes them to suffer the unspeakable upon coming to this city or any other in the United States.

As soon as Skinenbones saw Policarpo making himself comfortable, he rolled up underneath the bench on which Policarpo had stretched out. Policarpo let out a sigh that pointed down to the earth; and, to disguise the smell, he took out his little tin of tobacco and the booklet of papers, and twisted another cigarette to puff on and blow rings of smoke.

Immersed in his thoughts, and pondering how bad things are for his countrymen in these lands, he didn't even realize that night had already fallen upon him. But this allowed him to hear the melancholy toll of the churchbells of Nuestra Señora de Los Angeles, calling the faithful to pray the rosary with its chime.

Those big bells, which mean nothing to those who have lived for a while in Los Angeles, are very significant for new arrivals, who still have the smell of their native land in their nostrils. Despite how *macho* Policarpo was, his heart of hearts made him think about how foolish Mexicans are for leaving their Mexico to come to risk their lives in this country, where, with so many sacrifices and persecutions, one barely manages to scratch up enough dough to eat. The bells continued to sound, and Policarpo started to cry, without bawling, but, of course, with boogers hanging down from his nose.

As one of many tears fell, a fellow countryman next to him took notice and took pity on him: "Say, Jack, what gives? Are ya ill?"

"It ain't nothin', pops," answered Policarpo, trying to conceal his pain.

However, upon seeing someone had spoken to him, he didn't squander the opportunity to ask for his advice and make a friend who might be able to help him in some way—if not with money, at least by giving him the lowdown about some job. So, putting on a happy face, Policarpo took out his tobacco tin and offered him a cigarette.

Policarpo's new friend didn't make him ask twice; and, while they rolled their smokes, they started into a lively conversation.

"Tell me, mister," asked Policarpo, "is there lots o' places ta get work in a town like this?"

"Well, looky here, kiddo, it's purty slim pickin's out here. There's so many people outta work an' they says it ain't gonna pick up fer at least a month er two. So where do ya hail from, partner? 'Cause from the look a things, you jus' fell off the back the turnip truck."

"Yep. I reckon ya could say that. I'm comin' from the section where I was a workin', but a buddy o' mine, who come wit' me, went an' got himself hurt. So I come wit' him, 'cause they done sent 'im to the hospital here. He's up there in that hospital right now. An' I come without knowin' where ta go, 'cause I don't know anyone. An' what's worse, I ain't got two pennies to rub together. Aw, shucks, I don't know what ta do, or where ta go."

While Policarpo was recounting his situation, his fellow compatriot was taking puffs on his cigarette, occasionally scratching his head, then going back to his smoke.

After thinking for a short time and while Policarpo was taking advantage of the opportunity to take a few drags from his fellow countryman's cigarette, the compatriot finally lifted up his head and told him, "Well, see, the truth o' the matter is that it's mighty difficult ta get a job. I'm pretty broke. An' I've got a fire in my saddle, too. But so's that you don't spend this night outten the cold, come sleep over at my place. An' we'll go a lookin' fer work tomorrah."

The offer that his fellow countryman made filled Policarpo with surprise and gratitude. So with joy and some embarrassment, he grabbed the brass ring that had appeared from out of the dark. And so that new friend wouldn't come to regret it, he told him, "Say, mister, if'n you do me this swell favor, I swears ta ya that I'll never forgit it. An' after I git a job, God willin', I'll repay the favor you done for me."

Without anymore chit-chat, Policarpo's new buddy invited him to hit the road for his place to stretch out their legs and get some shut-eye. On the way to his house, the new friend, who was named Cirilo, bought himself ten cents worth of pastries, called "donas," which made both Policarpo's and Skinenbones' mouths water. But Cirilo didn't give them anything until they reached the room. Once inside, he split the "donas" with them in equal parts, that is, two each, because they had given him three for a nickel.

Two "donas" weren't enough to even get started, but since there was nothing else to eat, they filled up with water. After puffing on cigarettes, they were filled with rapture as they digested their food. After such a vast and nutritious supper, and inhaling mouthfuls of smoke from each drag on their cigarettes, our heroes lay themselves to rest in the arms of Morpheus. But since neither man had put out his cigarette, the burn that they soon got on their fingers brought them back to life.

As sleep swept over them, the only thing that they did was take off their tire-tread *huaraches* and lay down lengthwise. And if they didn't remove the rest of their clothing, it was because, in the first place, they were summer clothes, and in the second, they didn't have enough blankets. So, making themselves as comfortable as they could, they got ready to spend the night imitating Skinenbones, who had been snoring like a baby from the moment that he had gobbled down his share of the "donas."

11

Policarpo and Cirilo passed the night uneventfully. They were happy
for the most part, dreaming about quesadillas all night long, perhaps
because their shoes were placed so close to their heads. At any rate, as
we were saying, they passed the night uneventfully, for even though
the environment was charged, there had been nothing more than claps
of thunder, but no sprinkles. Or, to put it a different way, in the room
there was a revolution of thunderous blasts and suffocating gas, but
they sustained no casualties. At any rate, our pals, a little groggy from
the effects of the revolution, woke up at the morning's first ray of
light—coming from the lightbulb, which had stayed on all night. And,
acting in accordance with what they believed, they sacrificed a little
sleep to get up early and go looking for work. As for Skinenbones, he
lifted his head and then returned to sleep.

Once they were ready to leave, they gave the order to march, but
not without first combing their matted hair with a little saliva, for their
beauty sleep had ruffled their feathers more than usual. And so, after
complying with this rule of personal hygiene, they opened the door, hit
the road at a double-time march, and went out into the street, followed
by Skinenbones, who was pulling up the rear. Our chums, who had
slept in a room with the light on, had gotten themselves out of bed
very early, according to them. But what a surprise it was for them to
see that the sun was now at its highest point in the sky, and the time
for looking for work had already passed.

Since the only thing which provoked them to look for work was
their tummies' demands, which at the moment weren't bothering them
in the least, they decided to head down the trail to the Placita and wait
until it was time to go visit their buddy, Don Chipote de Jesús María
Domínguez.

Not much time had passed after they had arrived at the Placita,
however, before both of their bellies began to ask for food, undoubtedly the result of the exercise they had done and the full digestion of

last night's supper. The two partners just stared at each other like sacrificial lambs.

It was one in the afternoon when, during one of Policarpo's laments, he let slip out, "If'n I jus' knew where ta collect on this here piece of paper that ol' buzzard called my *time-card*."

Those words seemed to light a flame under his comrade, who, jumping about, asked Policarpo, "What piece of paper? C'mon now. Let's give it a look-see. Take it out so as we kin cash it in and git ourselves some grub."

Policarpo took out the infamous slip of paper and showed it to Cirilo without delay. No sooner had he seen it than his friend told him that they were going to play keep-away, and hightail it to the Santa Fe "Deep-o," where that slip of paper would be worth its weight in gold in the Finance Department.

With these declarations, Policarpo began to see a cut of steak dancing before him. Licking his lips at the mere thought of it, he jumped to his feet. And accompanied by his partner, who wasn't going to let Policarpo out of his sight, they took off to the Sante Fe Finance "Deep-o."

Sucking wind, with their tongues hanging out, our partners flew like a couple of bats out of Hell, as much for the hunger which tortured them as out of fear that the office might close on them, and they would have to go without milk or honey until the following day. Notwithstanding their concerns, it was no later than two in the afternoon when they reached the office. On inquiring about who could help them out by cashing Policarpo's time card, they were sent right off to his office. Without any formality, they presented him with the slip of paper and told him to come clean with the loot.

The *gringo* attending to them gave Policarpo a funny look, then told him to sign a form, which he did not do, because he didn't know how. So he just drew an X. And after this ceremony, eighteen clams were shelled out.

Those of us who have set out for the infamous United States know what it means to be hungry and poor, then suddenly make a little dough. So you can just imagine the joy those poor fellows felt upon seeing the marvelous sum of eighteen dollars glittering in their hands.

The first thing Policarpo did, after delighting in the cash he had just received, was to ball it up in his bandanna and stuff it down his pants for safe-keeping. He immediately told his companion that they should shove off to gobble down as much grub as they felt like.

His partner took the lead, knowing he was going to get a handout. This time, Skinenbones would not pull up the rear. Once again, our partners went down First Street on their way to Main. There were a number of restaurants along the way, but they didn't want to set foot inside any of them, fearful that they would be thrown out. It is understood that Chicanos must know their place, as filthy and rotten as it may be, if they don't want to start any trouble.

Like a couple of devilish souls now knocking on Hell's gates, our compatriates came to the first restaurant on Main Street. And without fussing over menus, they each ordered *gringo*-style "hameneg," which in Spanish is known as fried eggs and ham.

In cases such as these, no matter how faithful a companion our dog may be, with us through thick and thin, putting up with all of our abuse, we always forget to order a little plate for him. But Skinenbones, who was not up for tolerating such things and was impatient from the hunger now tearing him apart, began to complain by way of barks and scratches when they hadn't given his order to the waiter. Skinenbones' protests weren't like those of the *braceros,* who raise up and strike and kick and scream without anyone paying attention to them. Upon hearing his first complaint, Policarpo asked them to also bring out some "hameneg" for Skinenbones. And when they finally saw their much anticipated food before them, they dove in like pigs to slop.

Now our readers can just imagine how hard and salty the dishes placed before the trio were. So I'll just say that, for a few moments, nothing more was heard than the thundering of teeth and the splashing around of tongues making room for the saliva to get to the "hameneg." As for Skinenbones, I don't need to tell you that, with a bigger snout and a longer tongue, in less that two shakes of his tail, he was already begging for more, because the portion they had given him was too meager for the bottomless pit that he harbored. But, as everyone was busy with their own tasks at hand, they didn't realize that his music had ended but he still had verses left to sing. And so, he tied down his innards and waited for a better opportunity to come his way.

For a long while, our pals didn't exchange a single word. Only their eyes saw that succulent feast disappear, as if by magic. And when they finally ran their tongues over their plates, as not to give the dishwasher more work, they felt satisfied.

After licking their mustaches clean, guzzling down a glass of water, and lighting up a cigarette, they got up, paid the check, and hit the road with the intention of going to pay a visit to their Chipote chum. Policarpo reckoned—and rightly so—that Don Chipote waited anxiously to find out what had happened to them. And so, pointing their noses in the direction of the hospital, they stepped on the gas to get there as soon as possible, because it was getting late.

They were already on their way when Policarpo realized that he hadn't brought anything for his sick friend. So they made a stop at the first store they came across in order to purchase something for Don Chipote. And when they left, they were loaded down with all the cigarettes, pastries, and fruit they could carry.

Like a love-sick rooster who hasn't seen his hen for days—that's how Policarpo acted when he came to visit Don Chipote de Jesús María Domínguez. It seemed like it had been a long time—he hadn't been able before to stop by his sick friend's room, say hello, and give him gifts. So when Policarpo finally dropped by, he did away with great pomp and circumstance and introduced Don Chipote right away to his new comrade in hunger.

The first thing Don Chipote said, after offering his respects to their new partner, was, "An' Skinenbones? What happened ta him? Have ya seen him 'round lately?"

To which Policarpo replied, to calm him down, "He's outside. It's jus' that they won't let him in on account o' he's a dog, an' all. But he woulda liked ta've come in an' seen ya. An' I'm sure he sends his regards."

Policarpo hadn't yet finished his statement, when Skinenbones, who couldn't bear to be left outside in the street and not see his owner, suddenly snuck into the room. And letting go with jumps of joy and barks of all sorts upon seeing his master, he demonstrated his happiness upon finding Don Chipote alive.

The dog still hadn't finished his cheerful display when a nurse entered, stick in hand, to punish the one who had slipped by without giving the high-sign. But Skinenbones, now scared out of his britches, bolted straight for his owner's bed. With a single bound, he hid himself next to Don Chipote, thinking that it was safe.

When the nurse saw that the dog had settled down beside the patient, he calmed down. But he had no other choice than to tell Don Chipote to turn the dog over so he could be put outside, because hospital regulations did not permit dogs inside the rooms.

Both Don Chipote and Policarpo were embarrassed by the scene that Skinenbones had made, but they didn't know what to do. The nurse gave them a look as if to eat them alive, and finally Policarpo summoned up all his courage and, turning around, said, "Looky here, buster, why don't ya jus' do us the favor of leavin' him alone. We're awready 'bout to beat it, anyhow. I'll take him when we go. An' I promise we won't bring him no more. Whaddaya say? Be a pal. Who knows? Some day we might be doin' you a favor."

The nurse better understood their forlorn faces than what they had actually said. And, putting down the stick he was swinging around, he calmed down and said, "Okay. But you need to get packing right away. If my boss passes by, he'll throw that dog out on his ear, and me along with him."

After making that announcement, the nurse took off. Policarpo let his tongue fly right away. As if in confession, he recounted to Don Chipote all that had happened to him and all he had done; he gave him the things he had brought and said good-bye all at the same time, promising to come around again the following day.

The other partner, for his part, did what he could to show Don Chipote how sorry he was for his misfortune And he told him that he wouldn't miss Policarpo's next visit.

Our partners were already at the door when Don Chipote shouted for them to come back. Skinenbones didn't want to get out of the bed, hoping to spend the night in the room with his master, whom he had been licking all over since he showed up, to demonstrate how much he loved him. However, since it was Skinenbones' fault that Policarpo had to scram before it was time, they had no other recourse than to pull him by his tail from under the sheets. And in this way, with a bark here and a bite there, they left the hospital.

12

The vicissitudes endured by all Mexicans, enchanted by everything that catches their eye in this land where they look for work, are no secret to those who are familiar with Los Angeles. They come, as they say, to strike it rich. And it isn't that the city doesn't have the resources to offer its inhabitants, rather it is precisely due to its size that there are so many people, because the majority of Chicanos pack their bags for Los Angeles to make a better life for themselves. The result of this multitude of *braceros* immigrating to Los Angeles is that they do little more than pluck the goose bare and raise the height of the tortilla basket; because those who have jobs to offer, upon seeing this horde, steel themselves and pay the *braceros* as little as they can. Because we workers never have much cash to begin with, necessity forces us to work for whatever they are willing to pay us. Thus, we are never able to get our heads above water.

Policarpo, who had come to Los Angeles just so his good buddy wouldn't be alone, also had the wool pulled over his eyes, as happens to all the Mexicans who come. The duo had been roaming the streets of Los Angeles for three weeks now, accompanied by Skinenbones, unable to find work. The more they tried, the more everyone insisted that they had no jobs. Policarpo enjoyed his first few days in the city, because he was able to stuff his face and just admire the *gringos'* ingenuity, which he told Don Chipote about each day when he came to the hospital instead of looking for a job. But once his dough began to run short and things started to look desperate, he looked for work with the passion of a newlywed. He always got the same answer, because there were enough Chicanos out of work to stop a steaming locomotive. All the while, our good friend, Don Chipote de Jesús María Domínguez, had been getting better; but the truth of the matter was that, as he admitted, he was loving every minute of his recovery time. His only concerns were about Doña Chipota and his little Chipotitos, of whom he had heard nothing. Despite the two letters another patient had written and mailed off for him, he had not received a single letter from back home. So only this worried him. As for the rest, not even his wound bothered him anymore.

The day finally came when the doctors told Don Chipote that it was now time for him to pack up his things and find somewhere else to stay, because they had already taken care of him for a considerable amount of time, and he was now ready to go back to work. Don Chipote, who indeed felt better and wanted nothing more than to leave the hospital and put himself back to work, told them that he would be out of there that very afternoon when his friend came to see him.

They discharged him that afternoon, and when Policarpo dropped by, Don Chipote told him that he was now free to go and make the rounds with him in search of work on the streets of Los Angeles.

Policarpo felt as though his spirit had rejoined his body on hearing this news, because he now had no money left over for another day. Since Don Chipote also had a time card to claim, he had a glimmer of hope that he wouldn't go hungry while they were looking for a job.

Don Chipote was telling Policarpo all about the news when a nurse came in with his bundle of clothes. The nurse gave the bundle back to him, asking him at the same time to remove the hospital gown. The nurse didn't have to tell him twice, because, in less than the blink of an eye, Don Chipote changed out of the gown. And the two chums pointed their noses towards the door.

They were already busting out of the chute like a couple of string-tied bulls, when Don Chipote remembered that one should never leave without paying his respects to the host. And desirous to conform to proper etiquette, he returned to the office, an act which served him well. For while he indulged his civility and gratitude for the sweetie-pie in the office, she took care of the slip of paper that she should have shown to the Supply, so they could send him back if they wanted him to return to the section on the *traque*.

Don Chipote didn't know whether that dame understood his thanks, but, he had a clear conscience for having done what good manners required of him.

While Don Chipote was entertaining himself in the office, Policarpo was getting worried, because he figured that the Finance "Deep-o" had already closed and that Don Chipote would not be able to get the money they needed so badly. So once Don Chipote came out, paying no attention to the fact that his friend had a bad hoof and was still limping, Policarpo grabbed him by the arm and made him run as fast as he could.

Our readers will no doubt want to know what happened to Skinenbones. And right they are. But they should know that the dog now had his tail between his legs since the fright he'd suffered during the first visit to his master, knowing he had no other recourse than to resist the urge which he had to see Don Chipote until he left the hospital.

Suddenly, Skinenbones was surprised to see his owner. He nearly went batty, dancing and jumping all over him. It was like he would eat him alive from the pleasure of seeing him. From what I learned later, his tail almost fell off from so much for his master.

Don Chipote, for his part, didn't hold back petting the one who had been so loyal to him ever since their departure from home. At the same time, Policarpo became desperate, worried that he would not be able to cash in on Don Chipote's time card. Policarpo explained the dire fiscal crisis in which they found themselves to Don Chipote, who, as soon as he was made aware of the problem, ran along side Policarpo pell-mell to get paid.

But Don Chipote couldn't move very quickly, and the office was already closed when they got there, even though the distance to the station wasn't too great. And, with the pitiful thought of waking up the next morning without a place to stay, they hit the road for the famous Placita to find a spot where they could spend the night, for they believed that they would surely be doing it under the starry skies.

Presently, they reached the Placita and took a seat, awaiting a miracle from above. But, for the moment, the situation was under control, because Don Chipote had stuffed himself in the hospital and Policarpo still had enough to buy coffee and "donas" for the two princes.

In the meantime, Policarpo explained all the surroundings that Don Chipote was seeing for the first time, for these things were now commonplace for Policarpo.

As the Chicano community is very fond of knowing things that shouldn't concern them, there was no shortage of people who, upon seeing Don Chipote a little gimpy, asked him what had happened to him. And, naturally, he recounted the whole story of his mishap to them from beginning to end, and finished up by saying that he had just gotten out of the hospital.

A fellow compatriot, after hearing the story, asked if payment for the injury had already been arranged, to which Don Chipote replied that he didn't know they had to pay him anything. They had given him a piece of paper so that he could collect his check, but that was for the days he had put in on the traque.

His new friend told him, after taking a look at the slip of paper, that this was his time card and that what he had to do was to go see a lawyer, so that he could help him straighten out the matter, because the company surely had to compensate him for his injury.

The scoop given to Don Chipote by his new buddy made him wise up and made him want to get a little something for his foot, that is, with interest. He asked his compatriot how much a lawyer would cost, because he didn't have any money to pay him. His counterpart assured him that a lawyer would take his case and fix it so that he would pay him after it was all done; if he wanted, *he* could take Don Chipote to a guy who would swing this kind of deal for him. Don Chipote responded in kind and accepted his offer at once, promising as always that he wouldn't be ungrateful, and that, God willing, he would give him a little something after the case was won.

After his comrade took off, our partners remained immersed in their meditations for some time, undoubtedly looking at the stars, pondering the immortality of the Crab, and thinking about how far away they were from their families and homeland. Meanwhile, Skinenbones had also found himself a partner of his own, of the female persuasion, and entertained himself by courting her to see if he could win her over and whip out the conjugal lasso. But the little bitch, no doubt brought up according to American custom and not speak a word of Spanish, didn't understand the barks that Skinenbones aimed at her. She strung him along beautifully, while Skinenbones began to drool and pant upon seeing that she didn't seem to understand what he wanted. He did not understand that the doll-face he was after was just testing his love, so that after he gave her his heart completely, she could award Skinenbones with all that he asked for.

Our expatriates didn't realize how madly in love the dog had become. For, as engulfed as they were in their own thoughts, they didn't give a straw about puppy love.

The sun had already descended on the western horizon, and the first shadows of night spread their cloak over the knavish world, inviting it to go to sleep in the arms of Morpheus or whoever it may be. Skinenbones had already given the time to his bomb-shell pooch, the mistress of his doggy affections, when our heroes got up to check where the lovers had gone.

Because Policarpo already knew his way around, he took hold of Don Chipote and headed towards the "posoffes" on Main Street. Meanwhile, Skinenbones threw loving glances at his sweetheart, who licked him at the same time, then licked him again, as if telling her departing love that he didn't have to pay rent to stay where he was living. For his part, Skinenbones didn't stop looking at her until a transient's foot brought him back to reality. And with a yelp and a cry, he used in vain the name of the female progenitor of his days.

Our partners, like anyone with nothing to do, went counting their steps and stopping at all the storefront windows, drooling at all of the things they wanted, like the undergarments and the shirts, because theirs were now wearing so thin that they were afraid that if they took them off, they would simply disappear—and, because of their perpetual waterfall of sweat, they knew they were like a walking pestilence.

The more they saw, the more they liked the things, which seemed so inexpensive that they wanted to buy them, not just for themselves but for their families, as soon as they found a job. But since you don't have to pay for browsing, they continued to slobber in front of all the store windows.

Step by step, they made it to the "posoffes," or post office. And, because they now felt like the big fishes that gobble up the little fishes, they decided to go to an eatery that looked less crowded. Of course, calling it an eatery occurred only to Don Chipote, for Policarpo, who was already civilized, explained to him that these were called "resorans." And after making this observation so as to remove the stars from Don Chipote's eyes, they went in to get a bite to eat.

Policarpo immediately put on the airs of a know-it-all. And wanting to impress Don Chipote with the bit of English he had already learned, he made his order this way: "Gimme cofee an donas." When the waiter asked Don Chipote what he wanted, he just stared. But his partner was ready and said, "Gif im sem tu, ju no," with which he was handsomely rewarded for his wisdom, as Don Chipote was amazed that his chum learned so much in such little time.

Their desire for the scrumptious morsels knew no end, and our partners shoveled in bite after bite as Skinenbones desperately scratched at them. So they threw him a few scraps just to get him to stop bothering them. This was something the poor dog didn't like one bit, because he was very tired after his affair. In short, upon seeing how his owners chiseled him out of his share, he decided to take off in the direction of the kitchen, from whence came an aroma which nearly made him faint. And familiar with the doggy saying that the dog who never leaves the house, doesn't get the bone—or in other words, nothing ventured nothing gained—he disappeared from his masters' sight to see what God would provide for him.

Our pals, fearful that their partner, Skinenbones, would turn back around and get them into trouble, paid in a big hurry and scrammed before the roof fell in on them. They had barely gone a few steps out of the restaurant when Skinenbones caught up to them, carrying a sublime chunk of half-chewed hot link in his snout. Our chums seeing this and starting to hightail it all over again happened all at once. But since Skinenbones couldn't figure out why they wanted to leave, he picked up the pace as well. So as soon as they reached the Placita, the dog showed up and deposited the fruit of his mischievous labor at their feet.

The dog almost winked at them, as if to say, "Come an' git it!" And, to tell you the truth, their eyeballs nearly popped out of their heads at seeing all that meat, as Skinenbones just waited for them to join in on the banquet.

Our heroes, who hadn't filled up on the "donas" that they had pushed back, didn't spend much time contemplating the meat before tearing into it. So, after giving it a washing, they split the frank into two equal parts, giving one half to the dog and sharing the other between themselves. With this little bite, they squared-up to pass the night.

After they had polished off such a supper, and as it was already cooling down and the doctor had recommended that Don Chipote not stay out in the cold night air, they thought it best to shove off for somewhere to get some shut-eye. They did so, huffing and puffing to that rat-trap hotel where Policarpo had already rented a room, to see if they'd give them a hand by allowing them to stay on credit.

Entering the room, after obtaining credit, they removed their tire-treads, then their clothes, so, as not to wrinkle them. And, after saying their prayers, they went beddy-bye.

Don Chipote missed the hospital's accommodations very much. Notwithstanding, he slept like a log all night long. And, with no reason to get up early, he would have kept right on sleeping had it not been for Policarpo, who, knowing that the early bird catches the worm, got up very early in the morning, cutting short Don Chipote's sweet dreams.

After saying their morning prayers, each got up and gave a pass with one paw through his matted hair. They set sail for the Placita to wait for their fellow compatriot, who was going to take them to the lawyer who would arrange for them the compensation for Don Chipote's injury.

A watched pot never boils, and it seems even worse if you take into account that they had empty tummies. But a man must always keep his appointments, even when one is made between two Chicanos, who are famous for their lack of punctuality. Their pal showed up at nine o'clock sharp. They said hello, shook hands, and went for a stroll to the office of the infamous lawyer for Mexicans.

Because our heroes went with empty bellies, they were now seeing stars. And without anything to eat, they just stared at each other. Finally, they couldn't take it any longer, and they asked their companion if he wanted to go cash in his time card first, because they didn't have any loot to pay the lawyer if he asked them for something in advance.

Their comrade said no, not to worry, because even if he did ask for an advance, they shouldn't give him anything; as they say, "A musician paid in advance always plays a lousy tune." Our chums dropped their heads. But, in the end, they couldn't bear it any longer, and Don Chipote said, "Well, ya see, mister, ta tell ya the truth, if'n we don't have ta give that fella nothin', our bellies are still achin' 'bout what we ought ta have given them this mornin', 'cause we haven't given them nothin' ta work on."

Their fellow countryman, of course, understood that they hadn't eaten anything, so he no longer opposed going to cash in the time card. And they hightailed it to the finance station.

On the way, Don Chipote saw dancing before his eyes the slices of buttered bread that he had enjoyed in the hospital. So when he cupped his hands to receive the fistful of pesos paid to him, Don Chipote felt his spirit return to his body.

Naturally, they didn't take the time to think, rather they just let themselves go to replenish the void they felt in their stomachs, which was making them feel weak. That's how, then, they entered the first restaurant that they saw and dug in.

Satisfied with the feast, in which Skinenbones took part as they offered him a small plate, and now invigorated to fight the injury case, they directed their steps to the ambulance chaser's office.

In Los Angeles there exists a class of two-bit hooligans, who, strangers to the notion of working for a living, occupy themselves with picking the pockets of innocent compatriots who seek their help because they don't speak English. Such shifty-eyed rapscallions have established offices where they promise to arrange all manner of business. There are even fortune-tellers who claim to win the love of a woman through hocus-pocus. Others do translations, write love-letters and promise a thousand other absurdities simply to shear the Mexicans, who fall like lambs into their clutches. For some unknown reason, the authorities in Los Angeles don't purge the city of this plague of good-for-nothing loafers which grows with each passing day. They just give them an occasional scare, which never manages to get rid of them. The person writing this has had opportunity to meet a number of people who have been swindled terribly by these cons, who handle cases more or less in accordance with the law. Our countrymen have always been hustled and then rejected whenever they have tried to seek justice.

And it was to one of these crooks that their buddy brought them, only because he had once fixed it so that he would get paid for some time he had worked. He thought this legal eagle was the salt of the earth and a doer of good deeds for Mexicans.

After the introductions, the trio told him what the case regarded and about Don Chipote's claim. And the crummy lawyer, as soon as he got a whiff and saw that he could make some dough, talked them into sticking around.

He explained how they could make a fortune from the company, because the injured party had the right to who-knows-how-much. In short, he entangled them in such a net that our pals were sure that, with what Don Chipote could get for his injury, they would have enough loot to return to their homeland, buy a few teams of oxen, and go to work for themselves. Policarpo was so sure of what that fink had told them that he was even jealous of his partner and wished that he would have been the injured party.

Don Chipote, who had a full belly and a happy heart, plus the hopes that they had given him, was jumping for joy. He ran out of there ready to bust. So as soon as Cirilo saw Don Chipote's good fortune, being as how he made his living off others—after all, he was one of those Chicanos who goes looking for work praying to God he will never find it—he invited them to New Nigh Street, where there were places which sold wines which did not intoxicate, he said. It was called "si-dah." And there were a lot of dames on this street, to boot.

Our heroes, a couple of first-class suckers, allowed themselves to be convinced by their friend, who was already walking away from them. So they set out for the street which he had recommended so highly.

It didn't take them long to arrive. And, without further ado, as if Cirilo were going to pay, he ordered a few glasses of the "si-dah" which they had heard so much about. Once served, they drank up, toasting to the success of their case, which rested with the lawyer.

Our partners, foot-loose and fancy-free, let loose with the booze which didn't get people drunk. Gulp after gulp, they made room for it in their gullets, now and then lighting a cigarette for a little flavor. Since it's always more work to get started, and this guy easily got them going because of their own desire, they very quickly asked for another round, then another. They continued in this manner until they lost count. Although their tag-along had told them that "si-dah" would not go to their heads, shortly after throwing back those first rounds, they began to feel the world spinning and they couldn't contain their glee. And since we don't give a hoot or a holler about anything once drunk, the poor partners began to make a thousand funny gestures and became the laughingstock of all those who saw them. The drinks kept coming, one after another, making everything swell. Then Policarpo began to shout "¡Viva México!" and "long live" the patron saint of his *pueblo,* while Don Chipote was overcome with sadness and began to remember his family. Naturally, he gave free rein to his feelings, and with tears and snot running down his face thought about his beloved Doña Chipota and his little Chipotitos, of whom he had heard nothing, for she had not sent a letter in a very long time.

Luckily for our fellow countrymen, the exit was not very hard. Because they had eaten too much, their guts soon swelled like balloons and had no more room. They soon stopped drinking and lay down on a bench for a nap. After a little sleep, they woke up almost in their right minds. Their chum wanted to keep them drinking, but Don Chipote said no. So, leaving the *cantina,* they headed out to get a little chow, then go to bed.

13

In the morning, after washing their mugs and completing their morning routines, they left to go gobble down something to quiet the hangovers they were experiencing. So they went to a Mexican restaurant and threw back a bowl of *menudo,* very much to the delight of Skinenbones, who attacked the bones to the point of leaving them bare, even more than what his owners had left them. Later, Policarpo decided to go look for work and asked his pal to loan him a little something for food in case he landed a job. Then he told Don Chipote to meet him in the hotel room in the afternoon, because he wasn't coming back until he found work. After Don Chipote gave him a dollar, Policarpo beat it, and Don Chipote found himself on Main Street, looking around to figure out which way to go.

It didn't take Don Chipote long to get his bearings. He went to the Placita, because he didn't know where else to go. Also, there he was sure to come across fellow countrymen who could speak to him in his own tongue. He had already spent the greater part of the morning there, sleeping and smoking, until it appeared as though he was getting drunk again. In the end, he was getting bored and extremely sunburned.

Not knowing how to kill time, he thought about taking a stroll along Main Street. So he hit the pavement, just to rid himself of the doldrums.

That's how, step by step, he happened across a movie house and went inside, drawn by the comic always posted at the front door to lure people inside. The announcer was shouting himself hoarse, yelling about the attractions, which according to him were the season's best, and that they had the best movies ever. He was practically shoving passers-by into the theater by force.

Don Chipote, who couldn't find anything to do and excited by the announcer's spiel, asked how much a ticket cost. After finding out that it only cost ten cents, he bought his ticket and went inside to be entertained.

Skinenbones, upon seeing his master go inside and realizing he didn't even buy him a ticket, chased after him so that he too could watch the "sho."

Never in his life had Don Chipote seen a cinematographic projection—that is to say, he didn't even know that the "sho" would be in the dark. So when the house lights grew dim and he couldn't see anything, he wanted to run out of the theater, for he thought that he had descended into Hell. And with the lights completely dark, he couldn't see where he was going and smacked into one of the pillars in the auditorium.

Skinenbones caught up to his owner. But Don Chipote didn't want to let go of the pillar that he had run into. Skinenbones whimpered as Don Chipote's knees knocked.

Little by little, his eyes finally adjusted to the darkness and he began to make out the seats and everything around him. Once he could get a good look at things and see well, he took to the aisle. And without looking at where he was sitting down, he plopped himself down before the silver screen. It wasn't until Don Chipote realized that the fellows who appeared on the big screen were moving on their own that he began to get nervous; or more clearly stated, he started to get scared. So he made the sign of the cross, entrusted his soul to Divine Providence, and prepared to make a dash for the exit. But he stopped, thinking that he might fall while running and, that after he fell, they would do him in.

In the end, he decided to just bow his head and not look around, praying that Our Lady of Perpetual Help would get him out of this fix.

He had already spent some time with his head down beseeching God's grace, when a cry of laughter grabbed his attention away from his predicament. Unable to withstand his curiosity, he lifted his head and watched the screen as a funny-looking actor threw a cake at an old man but hit his girlfriend instead. The rest of the audience continued to laugh at the lunacies which comprised the comic scenes. Don Chipote felt the blood rush back into his veins, and also felt like laughing at those wise guys' shenanigans. It didn't take long for him to let fly with his guffaws and for him to shake the room with his chortles, which called the attention of the others, who, now being entertained by watching him, stopped watching the screen to laugh at Don Chipote instead. He thought that those pictures were so hilarious that they made him want to laugh even harder than he had on his honeymoon, when his Doña Chipota had tickled him in the morning so that he would wake up laughing with her, which made him fall more deeply in love.

Don Chipote then confessed to himself that he had no reason to be scared and that his fears were the seeds of his ignorance, because he now realized that, if he were being dragged down into Hell, they wouldn't have made him pay first. Once pacified by this thought, he occupied himself with watching the entertainment on the screen. And so that Skinenbones could see too, he picked him up and placed him on his lap and showed him what he was looking at. Of course, the pooch didn't give a straw about what was making his master laugh so hard, but he felt swell sitting on his lap, because it had been a long time since Don Chipote had so much as pet him.

Don Chipote, all the while, kept rocking back and forth with laughter, giving the others in the crowd reason to laugh at him.

While he was still laughing at the screen, and the others at him, the movies ended and it was announced that the variety show was to follow shortly. Even though Don Chipote had no idea what this was, he remained seated, only because the rest had stayed put as well. He began to get annoyed by so much waiting around, when to his delight, he saw a musician with a drum make himself comfortable next to the piano. And he thought, without a doubt, that they were going to dance the *matachines* like back home.

The piano *maestro* arrived at last. After giving the keyboard a few general passes, he attacked the piano furiously, in harmony with his sonorous companion, playing the *pasodoble,* which even the local barn owls recognize as *"Sangre Mexicana."* After they thought they had played the tune, for in reality nothing could be heard except for the drumming and crashing, the curtain rose and a dame appeared wearing almost nothing at all, making Don Chipote cover his face, which turned red from the embarrassment of seeing a woman in such regalia. And don't go thinking that this was false modesty on the part of our compatriot, for as you well know, in his homeland, he had never seen the body of any woman—dare we say, not even his wife—higher up than the ankle. So you can just imagine what happened to him when seeing that doll-face showing off her legs to the crowd, looking more like streams of *atole* than legs.

Because temptation is the worst thing that mankind can face, enabling the devil to take us away, Don Chipote could not resist. And, little by little, he went opening his fingers to see what would startle him once more. And that's how, little by little, he continued until he peeled his hand from his face straight away and began to study the beautiful performer and even drool with delight.

When the dull monotonous singing had ended, Don Chipote's sweet temptress gave her thanks and took off. People in the audience stomped their feet, yelled out loud and applauded. And our pal, corrupted by the others, cheered until suddenly standing up and letting Skinenbones fall from his lap with a crash, for he could not resist joining the tremendous ovation without howling his approval, which redoubled the cheers, because the crowd thought that it was the performer who had started singing again from the middle of the song.

The poor song-and-dance gal was not the greatest, but for the Mexican masses before her, she was out of this world, especially for Don Chipote.

The singer let the crowd go wild for a few moments, then decided to repeat the number, only, this time—and you should understand that what really made the audience go bonkers was the exhibition of her scrawny chicken legs—she sang and danced while trying to reveal herself all the way up to where her bloomers were fastened. With such an artistic display, the reader can imagine how the crowd must have reacted, particularly Don Chipote, who was going blind with ecstasy. Fortunately, now that he had nearly lost his sight, the artist wrapped up her routine and exited the stage to the cheers and stomping feet of the audience which wanted her, at all cost, to do more of the same.

The pack of Mexicans went rabid. They shouted and did all they pleased and could do to compel an encore, but that piece of eye-candy didn't come back out. Instead, a guy dressed like his compatriots in the audience—who had taken their turns with distilled cactus juice—attempted to win their praise as well by telling them jokes and babbling baloney as dirty or more bawdy than his predecessor's songs and legs. In short, that buffoon gave them a kick, not so much from his jokes, but rather because the pantomime he did made them recall getting hooched up back home. And that's why they awarded his evil deeds with a salvo of applause, which he received while doing cartwheels off the stage, his heart full of gratitude for those who knew how to recognize his talents so warmly. Surely, he thought they would make him do an encore, but as soon as he was out of sight backstage, the clapping came to an end.

Another number followed; rather, it was basically the same, only, this time, both performers came out on stage. The woman was now dressed like a country girl and the comedian just as before, only this time he didn't have on his *huaraches* and instead carried a *charro's sombrero,* which in its day had been braided with gold, but now shone with a mountain of sequins embroidered onto it. In these get-ups, our artists engaged in a street dialogue which they presented as a novelty but even children know it by heart.

Following this lovely exchange, in which they exhausted their vast repertoire, the *maestro* started in on his piano with thumps on the keyboard, sending out the discordant chords of the *"Jarabe Tapatío,"* while the artists *par excellence* started more or less into stomping their heels and kicking their legs to the music.

The row created defies description. The dust cloud cannot be described either, for, with each one of the dancers' steps, enough dirt came out of the slits between the stage's floorboards to build an adobe house.

The horde of Mexican performers who entertain in the United States know that the Chicano community goes crazy when something reminds them of their blessed cactus land. And, naturally, they exploit it all the time. Thus wherever there are theaters or even the humblest stages, whether the performers are good or bad, there will always be a drunken tramp with or without a *charro;* and if a comic goes to one of these places and doesn't know how to do the penniless tramp and dance the *"Jarabe Tapatío"* he will be deprived of a contract and presumed to be a Bohemian.

My readers will forgive me for introducing them to both the good and bad of the Los Angeles theatrical ambiance. But my little aside was only to give the performers, who continued to dance the *jarabe,* the opportunity to finish, while at the same time allowing the dust cloud to clear.

After Venus and the funny-guy completed the required steps, the audience was in the aisle with applause and whistles and cat-calls, as was the custom. The show was over and the curtain came down. The theater went dark. And then, the movies continued.

Some of those attending the performance got up and left. Others stayed in their seats. As for Don Chipote, he didn't know what to do, whether to stay or to go. But noticing that no one said anything to those who remained, he made himself as comfortable as he could and started to watch the movie, which he didn't understand, but which entertained him very much, just because the pictures moved as if they were real people. And all the while, Skinenbones snored away at his master's feet.

Not to make this story longer than it already is, I'll just tell you that Don Chipote got completely involved in the movie and then watched the variety show a second time. He would have certainly stayed there until they kicked him out, were it not for Skinenbones, who showed signs of boredom and hunger, making Don Chipote notice that his stomach too was now empty and starting to growl.

Thanks to this, Don Chipote abandoned the theater at last and went out into the street, somewhat surprised, thinking—the result of course of having been in the dark for too long—that the world had been painted yellow.

Since food was his reason for leaving, he went straight to the restaurant that he liked so much, which made the dog happy, because he was already making room in his little doggy gut. After gobbling down a few morsels, they burped, picked their teeth, and did what one does after eating a meal, then directed their steps to the hotel room to wait for Policarpo.

14

After a full day of merry-making and stuffing himself, Don Chipote felt like taking a *siesta*. So after getting to his room, he spread out on the bed and closed his little beady eyes.

Skinenbones too, as full as his master, rolled over and sprawled out lengthwise and went to sleep, to dream about his amorous affair with the dog from the Placita.

How long were they snoring? No one knows. But they woke up when Policarpo made his entrance.

Let's back up our story a little to find out what had happened to Policarpo after he left Don Chipote.

As we said before, Policarpo decided to look for work, even after tying one on with the "si-dah" he was drinking, after the hangover and the other happenings. He believed with all his heart that he wouldn't go back to the room, until he got hungry, because he already knew that if he waited to get a job, he would surely starve to death. However, luck was smiling on him, and after much hustling through the populous city of Los Angeles, he took his bag of bones to a construction job, where they were filling up the frames of walls with mixed cement and crushed gravel.

Cement work is not very desirable, and most workers only get into it when they can't find something better and they are obligated by necessity. What is this little job like? Even Chicanos, who are not afraid of hard work, turn and run away from it. And quite often, many have put in a few hours, or even an entire day, and still don't come back for their paycheck.

Policarpo came across this swell job by chance. As soon as they asked him if he wanted a job, he said yes. And without any further ado, he started working enthusiastically, as if it meant he could now eat.

It didn't take very long for Policarpo to find the work difficult because the machine that crushed the cement never stopped. The big cart he used to haul the cement in was soon wearing him out and making him hungrier. Fortunately, when he was just about to have a fainting spell from exhaustion, it struck twelve, as much on the clock as in his tummy. He went to go have lunch, which gave him time to rest and get himself up for continuing the work.

The other workers opened up their lunch boxes, or the wrapped bundles in which they kept their food, and began to gnash their teeth against what was contained within. But since Policarpo didn't have anything to refill his emaciated belly, he settled for just watching them eat and turning his tongue around in his mouth to let the saliva flow. Although he still had part of the dollar that Don Chipote had given him, he didn't know where he could buy food.

It didn't take long for the other workers to realize that the poor guy wasn't gobbling down a sack lunch. And, since they could see his eyes popping out of his head while watching the mouthfuls that the others crammed down, one of them came up to him and asked him why he wasn't eating.

"Well, my friend," replied Policarpo, "if'n I'm not grubbin' down on lunch, it's 'cause I ain't got none. But it ain't 'cause I ain't hongry."

The other worker, sympathizing with Policarpo's situation, offered him some of his own food, which he accepted right away. And so they divvied-up the goods "fity-fity," or rather, half and half.

After they finished with his ration, divided into two, his companion took out a smoke and offered it to Policarpo. They lit up, laid back lengthwise and began spewing out mouthfuls of smoke, when the clock struck one to get back to hauling the cart.

Policarpo was so exhausted from the short time he had worked that he might have wished that this break would never end. But, to his own misfortune, it didn't take long to hear the factory whistles calling the workers to return to their duties.

Upon hearing the whistle, all the workers sprang to their feet and, grabbing their shovels, carts and the rest of their tools, they went back to work with love in their hearts, waiting to call it a day. Policarpo, more forced than because he wanted to, took hold of his cart while his legs trembled at the thought of the drubbing which awaited him for the next three hours.

There aren't words to describe what Policarpo suffered. Although it was a job and he had spent his whole life working, cement work made him crazy as a loon, like everyone gets when they push a cart for the first time. Everyone watched him in amazement. He turned the cart over full of cement. The foreman yelled at him. He stalled getting in line to receive his burden. And, as if hiding in the grass, every once in a while he went to get a drink of water or to the toilet, as if what he had eaten were a laxative. Fortunately, the foreman realized that it was the first time that Policarpo had done this kind of work; and, very much to the contrary of the majority of foremen, he tolerated it without even thinking about docking his wages.

Policarpo was so worn out that he reckoned that all the clocks had broken their springs and would never reach four o'clock. So when he ventured to ask what time it was, he found out to his great dismay that it was barely half-past two. But he already felt like he had been working for an eternity.

He was following behind the cart almost unconscious and desperate when the whistle from the Pacific Electric streetcar brought the blood back into his veins. Hearing the whistle, letting go of the cart, and taking off happened all at once, for the poor guy believed that it was the factory whistle sounding four o'clock.

A "hey" from the foreman stopped him in his tracks. And with the face of a dead man, he turned to see that it was the trolley whistle that had made him make a run for it, thinking that it was quitting time.

The boss gave him a good thrashing for having thrown the cart aside and high-tailing it before it was time to go, but Policarpo took it, just like he took the teasing from his fellow workers.

Ready to die while hanging on to the cart, but not wanting to be the laughingstock for the rest of the workers any longer, Policarpo found his nerve and grabbed his little cart loaded with cement, believing in his heart that he was pure Chicano and would not give in.

As you all know, Chicanos for the most part are full of warm indigenous blood. And once someone calls their pride into question, or they call their own hearts into question, that's when they give it their all until they can't give any more. So Policarpo gathered up all the strength in his scrawny little body and continued "puchin" the little cart.

Now he paid no never-mind to whether it was four o'clock. So when the whistle finally blew and the others dropped their tools, our buddy kept on going until the boss stopped him.

When the energy of work had subsided and he took to the street, Policarpo cooled off and started to walk on his way to the hotel room. We can just image how he went: his legs bowed and trembling, his hands numb, bracing himself on the walls as he went along. In this state, he made his triumphant entrance into the room, where Don Chipote lay snoring with Skinenbones seconding him.

Don Chipote woke up and saw Policarpo in such a sorry condition that he asked Policarpo what had happened to him—had he gotten run over by one of those cars that run without oxen? Policarpo said, No, what happened to him was that he worked, and the job was hard.

Don Chipote continued to ask him more questions, but Policarpo didn't answer, because he didn't even have enough energy to speak.

Don Chipote began to tell him about the great time he had at the theater, thinking that this would lift Policarpo's spirits, but Policarpo didn't pay any attention to him. He removed his *huaraches* and spread out along the floor and immediately began to snore.

Don Chipote felt sorry for his companion. After considering that Policarpo didn't have any money and probably hadn't eaten, he thought about going out and fetching him something to eat for when he woke up, because Policarpo was certainly not going to move until the morning.

Don Chipote set out on his way to the restaurant where they had gone to eat that morning intending with all his heart to bring back something for his best buddy. Skinenbones, believing that another trap awaited him, followed his master. It didn't take long for our fellow compatriot to return with a bag under his arm, which contained Policarpo's sack lunch. When he went inside, he made the loudest noise possible so that Policarpo would wake up and see what he had done for him. But Policarpo was oblivious, so tuckered out that he had done nothing but snore since going to bed.

When Don Chipote realized how dead-tired Policarpo still was after his triumphant return, he went up to him and shook him around. He talked to him and did all he could to wake him up. But Policarpo just moaned and flipped over on his other side. In light of his failure, Don Chipote had a bright idea and put it into practice at once. Since he knew that Policarpo hadn't eaten, he emptied the contents of the bag and put it up to his nose. Oh, what a miracle! As soon as the nostrils on Policarpo's nose homed in on the smell of the chow, he woke up as if by magic. The grub he ate was just wonderful! I don't need to tell you the rest. You can already imagine it for yourselves. I'll just say that he dispatched what Don Chipote brought him in less than the blink of an eye and started to look around from side to side, as if an another package might fall out of the sky.

Don Chipote, grateful for his friend's loyalty, took pleasure in watching Policarpo guzzle down what he had brought him. Before Policarpo finished eating, Don Chipote had already given him water to finish filling his gullet. Policarpo drank until there was no more room. He then let out a burp which sounded like a cannon blast. He felt satisfied!

Rejuvenated by the gorging he had effected, Policarpo pulled out one of those boxes of Camels he had bought for Don Chipote and told him about the swoon he felt and how he didn't want to go back the next day. Don Chipote's eyes opened wide during the conversation, and it seemed impossible to him that the work could be so hard that Policarpo couldn't take it.

At Don Chipote's doubts, Policarpo told him, "If'n ya don't believe me, jus' go 'round those parts an' ask fer work. An' you'll see how you'll run away too."

Don Chipote felt his pride being challenged and he swore that, as soon as his foot was better, he would go ask for a job to prove that the work couldn't make him turn tail.

With this boast, Policarpo likewise felt put upon and decided not to miss the following day. So as not to stay up all night, after smoking another Camel, they stretched out and slept blissfully.

15

A few months passed.

Don Chipote's foot healed completely.

The little business that he had placed in the hands of the shyster was still unresolved. If the lawyer had collected anything, it remained in his own hands, and Don Chipote was left out in the cold.

After a few weeks of trotting through the streets of Los Angeles, Don Chipote landed a job as a dishwasher in a restaurant. And there we find him very well-fed and with some coins lining his pocket. Skinenbones is still with him and Policarpo. The dog is also very fat, dedicating himself whole-heartedly to his amorous rendezvous while his master provides for him.

After coming home from work completely worn out for the first few days, Policarpo gets the hang of his job and continues to work. So he too has a few "niquels."

Our pals believe that they must be in heaven, because Policarpo makes three-fifty and Don Chipote two-and-a-half dollars, in addition to getting free grub for him and the dog.

As they are now people with means, they have bought themselves get-ups like the other compatriots who come to the United States and make some dough. The duds consist of an aquamarine suit with lots of buttons, yellow shoes and a cowboy hat. And since bell-shaped slacks and tail-coats are so fashionable, of course they have bought those too.

Don Chipote, though he feels on top of the world, has not forgotten about his little Chipotitos and his beloved Doña Chipota, for he receives a paycheck every eight days and sends them a small part of it, which, at two pesos to the dollar in Mexico, allows the Chipote family to also live high on the hog.

In one of the letters that Don Chipote mails to his family, he sends them a picture he took in the street with one of those photographers who snaps them right then and there. Since he is dressed in his long slacks in the picture and wearing shoes and a neck-tie, his family does not recognize him right away. But after they figure out who it is, Doña Chipota shows the photograph to all of her friends so that they can see that her husband is a somebody in the United States.

In answering his letter, Doña Chipota asks him why he doesn't send for the family so they can be together and so that they too can buy such elegant clothes. But Don Chipote isn't thinking about bringing them over any time soon, because he is now after a flapper who waits tables in the same restaurant where he chows down. But he promises that he will send for them as soon as possible.

Another one of his daily pastimes is the theater, where the shows and the girls who sing and show off their legs keep him ga-ga. As for the rest, he's still a good guy and as naive as ever.

The proof we have of this is how worked up he is over the waitress, who, like all flappers, likes to fool around and is toying with him only to squeeze as much out of him as she can.

Don Chipote is hot to trot, and Policarpo's advice matters little to him. So, with each paycheck, after taking out what he sends to his little Chipotitos, he takes the flapper out for a good time.

After Policarpo's frequent warnings, Don Chipote has finally realized that the flapper is playing him for a sap. But since he is so worked up, he has asked for people's advice and they have given him the best: for him to see a good-for-nothing scoundrel—that is to say, a spiritualist, who cures all manner of infirmities without use of medicine, and who, because Don Chipote is lovesick, will surely cure him and will make it possible for him to win his flapper's love.

Don Chipote does not wait for them to repeat their advice. Without any further ado, he's off looking for this miraculous healer.

As soon as the witch doctor sees him, he knows that Don Chipote is his. So with thunder crashes and thousands of incantations, which Don Chipote doesn't understand (nor does the magician), he says to him, "Yours is a tricky one, but I can fix it for you. I assure you that you will win the object of your love."

Don Chipote doesn't realize that someone is pulling a fast one on him. Wanting to know how much the miracle will cost, he asks the price.

The witch doctor, who has already applied the meat-tenderizer, sinks his teeth in but tells Don Chipote that he will charge him only a moderate sum—for he, too, has been in love and feels the pain Don

Chipote is suffering. So, he'll only ask for one hundred pesos.

Upon hearing these words, Don Chipote's jaw drops to the floor and he stops breathing, losing hope of ever winning his flapper's love.

The soothsayer realizes this and he hastens to return Don Chipote to life, telling him not to worry, because, if Don Chipote doesn't have the money, he can still give Don Chipote something to begin the treatment, and he will grant him more with each paycheck.

Don Chipote starts breathing again. He sees the image of his flapper among the clouds, as the witch doctor licks his chops at the thought of how much he's going to bring in with this miraculous cure.

After agreeing upon the arrangement, Don Chipote pays him twenty semolians as a down-payment and the shaman instructs Don Chipote to bring him a lock of his girlfriend's hair, and, if possible, a garter and a shoe, because all of this is needed to make a concoction that she will drink and fall head-over-heels in love.

Don Chipote leaves the sorcerer's castle happy and sad at the same time; for though it is true that he is gaining his flapper's love (for one hundred pesos), it is also true that the ingredients to make the love potion are going to be hard to obtain. Getting a lock of her disheveled hair is easy enough. But how is he going to remove her garter and her shoe without her noticing?

With these love-swoons, Don Chipote is on his way to the restaurant to start washing dishes. At last! Oh, what a brilliant idea! He will give her a pair of shoes, a pair of stockings, and some garters as a gift. Then he will ask her to give him the old ones as something to remember her by. He has definitely nailed down a way to get the ingredients from her needed for the love potion.

———

Don Chipote arrived at work with this magnificent idea in mind. He removed his good pants, put on an apron, and started washing dishes while the kitchen boy kept an eye out for the angel of his love, who was coming and going, serving tables and doling out smiles to the customers, smiles that broke Don Chipote's crumpling heart.

That afternoon, after work, he put on his bell-shaped pants again. He gave a lick to the hairs sticking up so much that they wouldn't even allow him to put his *sombrero* on his head. Then, he set upon the restaurant owner. Without going into much detail, Don Chipote asked him if he would advance him a little something out of his pay for that week.

The boss, who had seen how hard a worker Don Chipote was and that he never missed a day of work, didn't hesitate to lend him what he asked for. And so, happier than a lark, our buddy went to go buy shoes, stockings and garters.

Now you can just image the dough that the poor man must have blown, wanting her old things at all cost, which made up the ingredients of the elixir of love that the witch doctor had praised so highly.

Poor Don Chipote! To alleviate his heartache, he went into a store, owned by some Jews, from which no one leaves without having bought something first, or enduring verbal abuse and the wrath of God. Since our hero had all the intentions of spending his money, the Jewish shopkeepers attacked him with kindness and nearly left him without a cent in exchange for the armloads of things they sold him. Don Chipote left very excitedly to give the presents which would undoubtedly open his flapper girlfriend's heart, presently welded shut, to his advances. In the meantime, Skinenbones, more fortunate than his master, had a crush on a number of pooches he had run into on the road.

Flying more than running into the restaurant where his flapper worked, Don Chipote sat himself down in the corner and waited for her to get off. Since she worked more hours than he did, he had time to wait for her to finish up.

For those who have fallen in love, it isn't difficult to imagine the impatience that our friend felt until his dame got off work. And don't forget that, like a bigshot, he was already picking up the language and calling his beloved torment his "gal."

As there is no time that will not come eventually, at last, it was time for his love to get off work. And it didn't take long for her to pack up her things. So in a few minutes, she appeared, and Don Chipote let himself go like a fox in a henhouse.

The flapper walked ahead of our hero, giving herself daubs of powder and jiggling herself from side to side. When he finally caught up to her, after falling behind as she strode off, he asked her, speaking with a honeyed voice, "Hey, where're ya runnin' off ta so fast so's I can't keep up wit' ya? Wouldn't ya like fer me to come wit' ya? What if'n I took ya to the 'sho'? An' jus' so's ta git ya a lil' interested, I'll tell ya that I got a lil' somethin' fer ya. An' I aims ta give it ta ya as soon as I kin."

She, who was only toying with him, but wowed him with the shake of her tail, didn't make him beg. Giving him a compassionate look, she told him, "Well, I guess I'll go with you, but only if you promise to be good. Because you already know that the 'sho' is in the dark . . ."

He, who was trying to beg this way, promised her what she asked, telling her likewise that she already knew that he was not one to make passes at a lady, and that she had already gone out with him a number of times, and he had never done anything to her.

So without further ado, he joined her, and the two walked together on the way to one of the "shos" on Main Street.

As soon as they arrived, Don Chipote rushed to get the tickets. They went into the theater, looking for the most isolated place in which to make their little love nest without anyone else taking notice, because Don Chipote was already burning up to give her the presents and to remove the old ones and take them to the witch doctor so he could make that infamous concoction.

Once they plopped themselves down, Don Chipote gave free rein to his passion. Stuttering from all the emotion, he told her that he loved her very much and that he had bought her a few things to try on, that the things he bought were not very expensive, but that he gave them to her as a symbol of his love.

As soon as the flapper heard "presents," her ears perked up. She looked at him tenderly. She drew close to him and glanced at the package again. Poor old Don Chipote thought he had ascended into heaven. At the same time, Skinenbones, who had never left his master's side and had snuck in without paying, did not stop staring at her and licking himself while remembering his own doggy adventures.

The readers must understand that Don Chipote, who had dressed to the nines, looked very *debonair*, in his own eyes. In reality, he looked just ridiculous, and had not stopped being Don Chipote de Jesús María Domínguez. The flapper, as you have seen, was not the kind of flea to jump into just anyone's gunny sack and was trying only to string him along. Even with the presents and everything he had done for her, and the witch doctor's plan, Don Chipote would never get anywhere with her. He was going to blow all his loot and the remedy wasn't going to work. Notwithstanding, he continued to be dogged in his determination, just like Skinenbones.

The reader must have also noticed that Don Chipote, because of his love affairs, was neglecting the Chipote clan in Mexico. This, of course, didn't sit very well with Doña Chipota, who was already starting to be on the lookout. If you add to this that Pitacio, who had stayed behind to care for the family, now wanted to go back to the land of the *gringos,* you will see that Doña Chipota was not extremely pleased that her husband would treat them like old shrubs.

As you will recall, when Don Chipote left his sweet home to try his luck in the United States (dazzled by the yarns which his pal Pitacio had spun for him), Pitacio stayed to watch over the Chipote family and the planting of the fields. Good buddy Pitacio was more than happy to do this—for the first few months. It was also advantageous for Doña Chipota that he left, even though she didn't agree with her husband flying the coop, hoping that he would quickly return after sweeping up all the gold in the United States with a broom. However, as the months went by and the news that she received from her husband was not good, she was the first one to write and tell him to come home, even if he didn't bring back anything with him, because Pitacio was not working enough, and the fields were going from bad to worse. Later, a letter arrived in which her husband told her that he was now doing well and working. It also contained the photograph that she boastfully showed to the whole *pueblo.* And this put her out of her skull, demanding that her husband send for her and his family. But, since Don Chipote had a crush on this flapper girlfriend, he didn't go through with it and just sent her some cash for food, promising her that he would return very soon and bring them the smartest looking get-ups they had ever seen. Doña Chipota was not convinced by all these wonderful promises, and she thought only about a way of reuniting with her spouse.

It didn't take very long for the opportunity to present itself, when

Pitacio told her that he was thinking about taking a spin for Don Chipote's parts, and if she wanted, he would send for her upon finding Don Chipote.

Doña Chipota turned over and over in her mind the idea of Pitacio sending for her when he got to where Don Chipote was staying. She reckoned that all men are the same and that the best thing for her to do was to go and take him along with her. When she was most set upon achieving her goal, she wondered how she could leave the little Chipotitos behind and where she could get enough dough for the trip.

Mulling it over and over, she finally decided to take all the little ones with her. To defray the expenses, she would sell the oxen, the plow and the rest of the farm implements. Thus determined, she looked for someone to buy her oxen as soon as possible. After selling them, she washed all the kids' things.

Everyone knows that it is easier to stop a river than a woman. So her family's advice, and even that of the priest, were not enough to change her mind. Once everything was sold, except for a few chickens for provisions, she gathered a good fistful of pesos and was ready. She believed she would go to the ends of the earth if that's where her husband was to be found.

Of course, she made all these arrangements without saying anything to Don Chipote, because she was sure that, if she told him that she was going to come for him, Don Chipote would tell her not to go.

The eve of her departure came at last, and with it, the execution of the chickens that would fill the Chipote family bellies during the journey. Some were made into tacos and as many of the others as possible were crammed into a large flour sack, which they had ready for the trip.

After doing all this, Doña Chipota asked Pitacio to go with them, since he wanted to meet up with his comrade. This way, because he knew *inglis,* he could do all the talking to Immigration. And in exchange, she would not bother him about the cost of the train or his food, because she had killed enough animals to eat and had sold everything so they would have everything that they needed.

In fact, with the sale of her things, Doña Chipota made enough for the trip. She didn't know how much the train tickets would cost, but that's why Pitacio was going with her. Pitacio didn't miss out on this opportunity to go to Los Angeles at no cost to him.

The day of the departure finally arrived. All the Chipote kinfolk gathered in the shack to bid farewell to the part of the Chipote clan which was blindly shipping out for the United States.

The send-off was very moving, as there was weeping and wailing, whimpering all over, fainting, and all that one has grown accustomed to seeing in such cases. In the end, Doña Chipota and Company detached themselves from the others and mounted a couple of donkeys rented expressly for the purpose of giving them a lift to the railroad station. The Chipote caravan departed, leaving behind the lairs where they had first seen the light.

Though Doña Chipota was used to riding around on mules and oxen, she had never set foot beyond the confines of the *rancho* before. After only a few leagues, she already found it uncomfortable on the back of her jackass. She carried the littlest Chipote in one arm and pulled a donkey by the harness with the other, and it was already twelve o'clock.

The rest of the little Chipotitos, who had horsed around at the beginning of the journey while Doña Chipota tried to set them straight by shouting, began to settle down, only to start up again soon with shrieks, asking to go back home, because they were tired. Doña Chipota, now in a devil of a mood, growled at one and yelled at another. But the one who paid the price was the poor mule, upon whom she unleashed her fury transformed into beatings.

As for Pitacio, not sweating nor overheated, he was absorbed in dreams of himself in bell-shaped britches in Los Angeles, and scarcely noticed Doña Chipota's temper tantrums.

So that the readers can see how the heavenly caravan marched along, I will give you an idea. There were four donkeys. Pitacio led the march on one. On another, Doña Chipota sat with the smallest Chipote in her arms, with riding gear, a few knick-knacks and fishing baskets, hanging from the sides, loaded with chickens for provisions. Three little heirs to the family name were on the third mule, one on the neck, another on the saddle bags and the last hanging from the tail. The jackass with the worst luck hauled a vast bundle of clothes— underwear, shirts, white petticoats, more underwear, a shawl for when Doña Chipota got dressed up, covers, more underwear, a bunch of diapers for the baby's needs, and a lot of dead weight—even Doña Chipota didn't know what was in there. That's how, as fast as a donkey could go, the family went its way to the United States.

It was around two o'clock in the afternoon when, as a result of their jostling mounts, they felt their stomachs empty. So the head honchos thought that it was time to open up the large sacks of grub and start eating. After pulling on the donkeys' reins, they made a stop under the shade of a few marmalade trees to worship the culinary faculties of Doña Chipota.

Naturally, they had empty stomachs because what they had eaten in the morning was already digested and ready to evacuate. So as soon as they set foot on the ground, they isolated themselves a little bit from the group to do what no one else can do for them. As for the little Chipotitos, they didn't wait to withdraw themselves from the others— they just deposited the precious bounty in their clothes. After they had done that, Doña Chipota had no choice but to put herself to cleaning them up and changing their clothes.

All the while, the donkeys, feeling the load off their backs, swung their tails freely and frolicked in the green grass.

Having completed the chores of bodily necessity and washing up, the horde rushed upon the large sack of chow, considerably diminished very soon. The kids, not waiting for Doña Chipota to dole out the food, stuck their hands in and stole as much as they could. The poor old lady screamed in vain and doled out one slap on the wrist after another. But despite all her yelling, they continued to grab at the grub.

To make a long story short, I'll just tell you that they ate most of their provisions. Then the mule driver reassembled his team of donkeys. Everyone mounted up as they were before and continued the journey, intent on reaching the town where the train went to Ciudad Juárez that same day.

Nothing worth telling happened to the pilgrims during the second leg of their trek, as Doña Chipota kept on shouting and frequently beating her poor donkey on the head; he continued to pay the price of the good lady's fits of temper.

It was eight o'clock at night when the caravan entered the *pueblo,* searching for an inn in which to stay. This didn't take much effort to find, the mule driver being familiar with the town. He went straight to the inn, where he requested lodging for the family and feed for the beasts of burden, although he didn't have to, because they had brought enough for everyone.

The Chipote gang arrived tired and hungry. So, after they laid out their sleeping mats in the halls of the inn, they opened up their sacks again to drain them a second time, nearly hitting bottom. Doña Chipota realized that the provisions would not last another day and thought it would have been better not to have sold any of the chickens and kept them all for food for the road. But since what was done was done, she had no choice but to just grin and bear it.

Once they tuckered themselves out, the kids bowed their heads and began to snore, while Doña Chipota paid the mule team driver, who had to return to the *rancho* the next morning after dropping them off where the train passed.

After paying him off, she looked for her own little spot. She placed herself next to one of her little Chipotitos, said her prayers, and after seeing that all of her little ones were asleep, she stretched out full-length, but couldn't sleep despite being completely exhausted. She fretted about the trip and everything that she had on her mind, especially that her husband Don Chipote was getting into trouble with his chums.

She finally fell asleep at who knows what time.

16

Like a good little farm girl, Doña Chipota woke up in the morning to the rooster's first cock-a-doodle-doos and the donkeys' first brays, accompanied by the mule driver's words from Hell's Dictionary, spoken to the jackasses that didn't allow him to sling on their riding gear.

As we were saying, the fair lady woke up and immediately began to get ready to continue the voyage. So as not to carry around more than what was necessary, she went out into the pasture, squatted down, and dumped what she had now been carrying around uselessly, for the beneficial part had already been strained out.

She then went to roust out the little ones, who promptly sprang to their feet. And after the order had been given, they too went to the field to drop a load. But the smallest one didn't need to go to the pasture with his siblings, because he had made himself lighter who knows how many times during the night, to the point that he looked like a violin in a puddle of water, as he was nearly swimming in his own juices. For Doña Chipota, this was nothing new, and, grabbing him by the feet, she washed him up. So, in less than two shakes of a baby's tail, she changed his clothes, but not without having first removed the encrustations with a little spit and a few rubbings with a baby blanket.

He was now ready. The rest of the flock showed up, now a little lighter. Pitacio, who got up as everyone was emptying their bellies, demanded some chow after making a deposit of his own.

Doña Chipota heated up the remainder of the provisions, which were shared equally among the masses and gone in less time than it took to serve them.

She then gave the order to march, and the caravan headed out, hauling their packs on their backs. Now the readers can just imagine how the family must have looked with so much dead weight as they crossed the streets of the *pueblo* on the way to the train station.

They finally reached the station. Sweating buckets, they put down their bags and headed for the ticket agent. Doña Chipota had no other choice than to have Pitacio ask the price of the tickets to Ciudad Juárez. Pitacio was happy to oblige, thinking he would have a little something left over to buy cigarettes for the road. Acting very much like a know-it-all, he went to the window and, without hesitation, spewed out to the employee: "Say, mister, how much does the train goin' up north cost?"

The agent replied, "Well, friend, we don't sell trains here. But we do sell tickets to Ciudad Juárez."

Pitacio, somewhat frazzled by the teasing, told him, "Well, that's all I was askin'. Be a pal and don't do nothin' else ta make me look bad in front of the lady."

The ticket agent, seeing that Pitacio was getting upset, hastened to tell him how much the tickets cost. Pitacio conveyed the price to Doña Chipota, along with his own surcharge. She broke out the dough for the tickets without further delay.

Once everything had been taken care of, they waited for the train, which didn't take long to arrive, but with it came new worries for the family, who searched hopelessly for room to accommodate all the parcel they had brought with them.

In the end, they made themselves comfortable. The train whistled, and they were off.

———

Nothing worth recounting happened to our pilgrims during their journey. Doña Chipota had planned for her journey with a handful of diapers. Her littlest Chipotito soon went through them all. And, one by one, throughout the journey, they were seen flapping out the train window, fully loaded with digested food.

Finally in Juárez, Doña Chipota put Pitacio in charge of arranging everything necessary for them to cross the border. Pretending to be an expert, Pitacio took off and stopped at the southern bank of the Río Bravo to watch how people crossed over. He thought this to be sufficient and returned with the news that he already knew where to go.

Without further delay, Doña Chipota ordered them to shove off, because she was already burning up inside to be with Don Chipote. With this, the horde headed straight for the bridge. With Pitacio taking the lead, they marched to the beat of the youngest Chipotito's screams. They passed the Mexican guard post with the wind to their backs. They crossed the bridge. And they would have continued on, if not for the *gringo* soldier who told them to halt and took them inside of the Immigration building. Our fellow countrymen, completely flustered, followed behind the other Mexican masses right into the shower room to wash away their sins before crossing into the United States, for there was no other way to get across.

Our chums saw everyone taking off their clothes, so they did the same. And Doña Chipota, who didn't want to take off her threadbare rags, was brutishly hauled away by a *gringa* who took her to the ladies' side, scolding her as they went for going into the men's shower. All of this went through one ear and out the other, because Doña Chipota didn't understand a word.

The poor lady's worries were innumerable. Just imagine how she must have looked while bathing herself and washing the herd of children that never left her side, day or night. However, it all seemed like no big deal to her when compared to the joy she would feel when she found herself in the arms of her beloved Don Chipote.

After they left the shower room and their clothes, newly fumigated, were returned to them, they discovered that the clothes didn't fit any more because they had shrunk with the heat. But since they didn't have any others—for the clothes in the bundles had shrunk as well—they put on their things and, with their hair still dripping wet, followed those who went into the immigration office.

After waiting all day, when their turn came to arrange their papers, they found out that they didn't have any of the documents necessary to cross the border. A *gringo*, already tired of working, rudely turned them away. Then a big *gringo* soldier took them, with great care and shoves, to the middle of the bridge with their noses pointed towards their homeland.

Doña Chipota thought that her world had come to an end when they denied her entry. No matter how much she stomped her feet or begged, it still didn't make any difference. So she stormed off, accompanied by the gang of little Chipotitos, to take possession of a spot under some shade trees on the bank of the Río Bravo.

Once they set up camp, Pitacio sat with his hands under his chin, the kids threw dirt clods at each other, and Doña Chipota tanned one of the little Chipotito's hides. Finally, they came together to figure out how to pull a fast one over on the *gringos* and sneak into the United States.

After much contemplation, now that the shadows of night had begun to make their presence felt, Doña Chipota awoke from her meditations, which were now converted into a fury against Pitacio. She told him that it was all his fault for having talked her into leaving; the only reason she brought him along, paying for all his expenses, was because she believed that he knew English and would take care of everything. And to cap it all off, she even told him that he was the one who had hogged all of the chickens that she had killed for food.

After this barrage, poor Pitacio couldn't even find a hole to crawl into, making him just want to buzz off and leave poor Doña Chipota on her own. But his belly made him take pity on her. Since he didn't have a dime to his name, he thought that if he separated himself from the one with the loot, he would be out of luck finding food. So he opted to stay.

The little Chipotitos had already started to pierce the air with their screams of being cold and sleepy when Doña Chipota ordered Pitacio to go find a cheap place to spend the night. Pitacio was much obliged and did so in a jiffy, because he didn't like the idea of spending the night under a tree. Leaving the flock, then, he went to find lodgings.

Pitacio finally returned with the news that he now had a place to stay for as long as they were willing to pay a dollar a day. But he needed to explain to her what a dollar was, because Doña Chipota was accustomed to paying with Mexican pesos.

After much inquiry, Doña Chipota decided to break out the two eagle coins and they went to the room, where they would later spread out to get ready to snore after eating supper. Pitacio had been sent to buy them some grub.

When Pitacio came back under a pile of *gordas, chicharrones* and cheese, they all attempted to devour everything at once. The chow didn't last long. And when big ones and little ones alike were so full that it even made them shine, they hit the hay.

They say "a full belly and a happy heart," but Doña Chipota, though very full, didn't feel at all happy. So it took a long time for her to close her eyes and finally begin to snore.

They slept like logs that night, which isn't anything unusual, if you take into account how exhausted they had become during the day.

Morning finally came. As the eastern sun lashed them with warm rays and the morning air filled their lungs with life, Doña Chipota complained about her destiny of having to wash the baby Chipote's backside, for he was practically swimming in the liquids he had saved overnight.

Pitacio got up. The other kids did the same. As they all completed their morning routines, Doña Chipota took responsibility for preparing the vittles to replace what the laws of nature had taken away.

We leave the family waiting for Pitacio to come with food, as we follow him, saying to Hell with going back as he goes wherever his nose tells him that there are pots of *menudo*.

Pitacio was not led astray, or better said, his nostrils didn't lead him down the wrong path. After a short walk, he came across a vendor selling *menudo* that looked from the greenness of its color like it hadn't been properly washed. It was the color of cow pies. Nevertheless, Pitacio asked them to serve him a bowl with a pig's foot. When he took possession of it, he began to gobble it down with a full complement of tortillas.

Pitacio was chewing away when one of those big palookas, who are only around in Juárez, sat next to him and sized him up. Looking at our man's hair and build, he started a conversation with him to see what he could get out of him. And he certainly didn't regret it, because he got enough from Pitacio to go without a care until coming across another chicken to pluck. It all went a little something like this:

Between mouthfuls, Pitacio told the *coyote* about the situation in which his friend's family found itself. And to top it off, he was stuck with the old lady, who was now telling him even when to eat.

That shark, hearing this, guaranteed that he would help them cross; it was one of his livelihoods, or so he said, for all these *coyotes* really do is point out the road for people to take on the other side of the river.

At any rate, Pitacio saw the heavens open up before his eyes and practically dragged his new buddy over to see Doña Chipota so that they could make a deal, because he himself could not get involved in the business end of matters.

When that derelict was introduced to Doña Chipota, she felt like a guardian angel had been sent to her from above. So she got down to business right away, but not without first asking Pitacio for the food, because the little ones were already crying for something to fill their bellies.

Pitacio said that he had forgotten due to the haste with which he had brought the angel, but that he would go back to get some grub while she arranged their crossing, and he took off.

There was no time to lose nor much to inquire about, because the guardian angel talked Doña Chipota into it in less than two shakes of a dog's tail, promising her that he would deliver them safe and sound to the other side of the border for the modest sum of five dollars a head.

Doña Chipota tried to make like when she went to the market in her *pueblo,* where she haggled until they lowered the price. But our man, who knew that she needed his services, didn't go down one cent, no matter how much she begged him to do it. So she presented him with the amount required to cross the border. And so, as we said before, the agreement was sealed in no time, and he took his leave, saying he would return to tell them what time they were going to cross. He said good-bye, but not without first taking a down-payment, that is, for the initial expenses, which Doña Chipota gave him with a "see you later."

As soon as he left, our guardian angel went directly to the *cantina* to celebrate the beginning of a wonderful day. That's where he paid the first expenses for the Chipote family's crossing, not waiting long to get himself as drunk as a skunk.

Not much time had passed since the *coyote* had left, when Pitacio showed up with a pile of *gordas* and pieces of tripe; since he didn't have a pot, he couldn't bring the soup, but so it would not go to waste, he had drunk it with another dozen tortillas that he put on the tab.

His arrival was met with great displays of joy from the Chipotes, who immediately swept like an avalanche over the food, which quickly disappeared without filling their bellies. But as Doña Chipota felt like celebrating, she gave Pitacio the order to go get another batch of *menudo* with an accompaniment of tortillas.

The day went by in the following way: Doña Chipota washed the baby's diapers, so that he would be, as they say, squeaky-clean for crossing the border; Pitacio went on a stroll to get the lay of the land, returning at chow time, only to leave again; and the kids made mischief to the point that the landlord gave Doña Chipota an ultimatum: Either settle her children down or get out of the house. This caused the kids to suffer at Doña Chipota's hands (on their backsides) all day as a consequence. But even with all of that, the pranks continued.

It was about six in the evening when the *coyote* appeared in more or less a state of drunkenness, saying that everything was ready for them to cross the border and they just had to wait for night to fall to start on their way to the United States, where, according to him, the streets were paved with gold.

That this bozo would show up in such a condition didn't sit well with Doña Chipota, but splashing them with water, she started to get the kids ready to move out. She was busy doing this when Pitacio arrived and received an order to assist her, which he did, thinking that the day wasn't far off when he would be able to get as far away from her as possible.

When everything was ready, the night had just cast its shadow.

So after they paid the rent for the house, they shipped out with the *coyote*, who was going to help them cross, leading the way. Staggering from one side to the other, he took them to the outskirts of town.

Who knows how long they must have walked? After scouting out the land, the *coyote* told them to wait for him behind a couple of bushes, while he went to check out the crossing-place. He instructed them not to let the little ones cry for any reason. And with this, he was out of sight, while the Chipote family stayed behind trying not to move even a muscle.

The *coyote*'s first thought upon leaving was to go throw back another snort so as to have the courage for the business that awaited him. But, putting his hand in his pocket, he discovered that he didn't have a dime. So without even thinking about it, he went back to Doña Chipota to tell her that he needed a little bit of money to be able to take care of some paperwork that he had forgotten about.

Doña Chipota didn't believe him, but since she was already into it up to her eyeballs, she came up with what he asked for and told him not to dilly-dally, because the kids were already sleepy and they probably wouldn't be able to keep quiet. He promised that he wouldn't take long. Without further ado, he hit the road for the city to throw back another shot. He headed once more to the first *cantina* he saw, forgetting all about the flock which he had left hanging out to dry.

When he finally polished off the booze they gave him, he thought about going to sleep, which he would have surely done, were it not for running into a friend along the way who asked him how business was. This reminded him of his contract. And, at a drunken trot, he went to the place where Pitacio and Doña Chipota anxiously waited for him, with their paws held over the kids' mouths or telling them stories so they wouldn't cry, until they had finally fallen asleep.

You can just imagine how much grief Doña Chipota gave the *coyote* when he returned. But he just let it slide off his back. And, asking them for the rest of the money, he told them that he was now ready to take them across. This earned him another round of abuse from Doña Chipota, who finally broke out the dough, hoping to see the last of that good-for-nothing loafer who was sucking up all of her cash. The *coyote* ordered them to march, stating that now their papers were in order and they could finally cross the border.

Having come to the edge of the river, the *coyote* told them to take off their shoes so that they wouldn't get them wet when crossing the river. Once Doña Chipota heard this, she rose to the tips of her chubby toes and started to holler at him, trembling with fury. She told him that they had agreed that he would take them across the border and that's what they paid him for. Then she asked where were the forms that he had said that they needed, now that she realized that they didn't need any papers, nor to pay anyone to cross a river.

The *coyote*, who was a real sharpie and knew that it was better to keep quiet in these situations, didn't say a word because he already had the loot. So he just let the storm pass. When the lady was through, he told her that it was all that he could do, and if they wanted to cross the border, to do it, and if they didn't, don't.

Doña Chipota, who saw that they had no choice, took off her sandals and ordered the others to do the same. Then they went into the river, even though they didn't want to, holding hands for their protection.

And so, in this way, and shivering from the cold, they crossed the border and found themselves in the infamous United States.

As soon as the *coyote* saw that they were in the middle of the river, he beat it, leaving them in the hands of their good or bad fortune, happy for having made enough dough to spread around.

When the group reached dry land, everyone fell to their knees, and on Doña Chipota's command, they gave thanks to God for having delivered them safely. They were in the middle of the prayer when they heard a noise. They sprang to their feet and beat it, afraid of being found out. So, without any particular path to follow, they plunged into American territory, headed for El Paso's lights, which served as their beacon.

17

Trotting along, our heroes strolled by Washington Park, precisely where the canal runs through it. Thank God there wasn't much water in it. Since the Chipote family didn't know where the bridges were, they reckoned that, instead of following the canal until its beginning or end, it was better to cross it now that they had already wet their footsies, and it wouldn't make much of a difference to get a little wetter. That's why, then, they removed their sandals from their feet with the goal of surmounting that obstacle. The canal had a steep drop-off and they had no other choice than to lower themselves down it. Pitacio took hold of Doña Chipota's shawl to support her as she cradled the littlest Chipote in her arms and slid down. In this way, they went down one by one, Pitacio's turn coming last to reunite with the group. Then the issue of climbing back up presented itself. Pitacio ignored the problem, quickly trying to hoist himself up by the cement ledge. And there he was, struggling to reach the top, without doing more than just clawing away in vain, unable to get to solid ground. In the end, he had almost drowned himself when it occurred to Doña Chipota to push him up and help him out of the mud hole. In this way, Pitacio was finally able to reach the top. And once up there, he began to pull up the others with the aid of Doña Chipota's shawl until everyone was finally on top.

Immediately after putting on their sandals, they started out on the long trek towards city lights, without coming across anything that might obstruct them on their way. When the sun started to rise for the comfort of those without blankets, they were upon the streets of El Paso, which pulls in Mexicans like a magnet, because this is where the employment agencies are located and where one finds his way on to the *traque.*

The Chipote family didn't go to those streets because they wanted to find jobs, for, after the night they had just spent, the last thing they wanted was work. On the other hand, they desperately wanted something to eat and some shut-eye. As a result, Doña Chipota parked herself beneath a doorway and told Pitacio to go and look for food and a place to stay. Pitacio responded that the best thing to do would be to go to a restaurant, where, for very little money, they would be given enough food to burst. Then they could go to the hotel to snore.

Doña Chipota, in no mood to argue, agreed. They then let their noses guide them to a restaurant. It didn't take long to find one. They went inside and took their seats.

As soon as one of the waiters saw them, he let them come in, and in English, he asked them what they would like to eat.

As our readers will recall, Pitacio had already been to the United States. Nevertheless, he didn't speak a bit of English and knew only how to order what the majority of us Chicanos know—that is, "jameneg," "stek," and "hocake." So, without beating around the bush, he asked for those three things, while looking over the menu first to give the impression that he was reading, which he couldn't even do in Spanish.

Doña Chipota was amazed at seeing how well Pitacio understood American. Her faith was restored in him after thinking that he was afraid to speak English. So after she asked him what he had ordered, and he explained it to her, she did not hesitate to order the same for everyone.

It didn't take long for their food to arrive, which surprised the whole family, who had never in their lives seen a table so full of such delicious dishes. So, not knowing where to begin and not wanting to look like nitwits in front of all the people, they decided to wait, as hungry as they were, until Pitacio started to eat, and then they did everything that he did. The first thing Pitacio did was to put the utensils to one side. They all did the same. In this way, with one eye on their plates and the other on Pitacio, they gobbled down their meals until they filled up their bellies, having struggled to eat as much as they could.

Since they weren't able to do away with everything, Doña Chipota, knowing the saying "Waste not, want not," and also knowing that the food was hers because she was going to pay for it, began to make little bundles with the leftovers, reckoning that they could make dinner out of that.

She was doing this when the waiter showed up and gave her a slip of paper with the bill written on it. And it wasn't exactly a jump for joy that she did when they told her how much it was. She would have surely made a scandal if it were not for a policeman who entered the restaurant—and Pitacio was there to tell her so.

Upon the sight of the flatfoot, Doña Chipota didn't make a peep. With all humility, she took out her money and paid. Then she went out into the street, cursing the overeating they had done, as well as the shooting pangs in her belly.

Now in the street, her eyes closed and half asleep, she told Pitacio to look for somewhere to sleep. Pitacio took them to the first hotel that he came across. They rented a room and in no time, nothing was heard except for their snoring, accompanied by one zephyr after another leaving the digestive tract.

They happily snored all day long. In the evening, the clan of Chipotes began to open its eyes, and in a short while, the whole family was up on its feet and ready for whatever God might decree by way of Doña Chipota.

The first thing she dictated was for Pitacio to go and see how they were supposed to get to Los Angeles, and to bring back something on the way for them to put in their gullets, because they were already starting to get hungry and would surely not be satisfied with just the leftovers from lunch.

Pitacio didn't make her tell him twice and immediately left to carry out her orders. But the first thing he did was to go to a restaurant and attend to his own belly, and he didn't leave until he was full. Then he commenced his search for their way to go to Los Angeles.

He took a great many offers, but since he didn't feel like making the trip in an automobile, because it would be very uncomfortable, he decided to pass by the train station to see how much the tickets would cost. When he made note of the information that he thought necessary, he went to buy some grub for the family, which jumped on him like pigs to slop when he arrived.

After they ate, Doña Chipota asked Pitacio about the matters that she had entrusted to him. Pitacio let her know that she would have to cut loose with enough pesos to pay for the tickets to Los Angeles, and that she had to change her Chicano dough for dollars, because the train station didn't accept Mexican money.

Doña Chipota nearly dropped dead upon hearing how much

Pitacio asked from her to buy the tickets at two for one. But she told him not to dilly-dally and to check if it was possible for them to leave that same night.

Pitacio left to see if someone could change the money. Since he was in El Paso, where there are many money-changing *coyotes,* it didn't take long to run into someone to take his loot in the blink of an eye. Pitacio, who thought he would get something back, broke out his stash, and almost didn't have enough to purchase the tickets.

He then returned to the hotel with the news that the train would be leaving in an hour and that they had to hurry up to get there to get a place before the train filled up and they would be forced to stand.

In less time than it takes for me to tell you, Doña Chipota prepared the necessities. And, at a trot, they directed their steps to the train station, making themselves somewhat comfortable after feeling a sweet sense of well-being in their posteriors on top of the velvety seats, which made them quickly begin to snore and give off Z's even before the train left the station.

Luckily for the Chipote family, the train which carried them was the one that they call the "expres." And so, when they awoke after snoring all night long, they found themselves practically midway through their journey. That same day, by evening, they found themselves in Los Angeles in the Southern Pacific Railroad Station. Loaded down to the bajeezes, like all the green Chicanos who come to the United States, they crossed the station beneath the eyes of the *gringo* railroad employees, who looked at them strangely. And in this way, their mouths wide open in amazement, they continued to drag their things along Fifth Street until they ran into Main, which is like diapers to flies for the Chicanos, because everyone seems to pick up the smell.

Once on this street, they continued north following the odor of the Mexican's Placita. In this manner, they came to the front of the post office, where Doña Chipota gave Pitacio orders to look for an inn where they'd put up for the night.

While he walked up the street, the family remained in front of the post office, huddled up together, one holding onto the other, for fear that someone might set upon them.

It was already growing dark when Pitacio arrived with news that he now had a place for them to spend the night. So, with everyone holding hands, they advanced in a row, following Pitacio, who stiffly carried all their things as Doña Chipota tugged at his shirt, because it was already midnight.

After two blocks, which felt like leagues to everyone, they finally reached the hotel and took it by storm, to the manager's delight.

Once in the room, it was transformed into a bullring, as the little Chipote clan started to become annoying with screams and shouts, some crying that they were sleepy, others that they were sleepy and hungry, others that they had to go potty, and all at the same time.

Doña Chipota was overwhelmed trying to attend to everything, and the first thing she did was put Pitacio in charge of getting some food. While he was gone in search of the requested meal, Doña Chipota multiplied herself to care for the horde of little Chipotitos, who nearly blew out her flame. Since she had no other option than to serve them like a good mother, she gave it more than her all. The crying continued at such a rate that the hotel manager had to go ask what the devil was going on, threatening to kick them out onto the street if they couldn't stop the racket. Poor Doña Chipota grew desperate—she had already taken them to the potty, but the little rascals kept on bawling, because they wanted food. In total desperation, the mother offered to breast-feed everyone, but the older ones refused, and only the smallest Chipotito went to her nipple like a leech.

At last Pitacio made his appearance. And, as if by magic, the screaming stopped. After stuffing themselves with what Pitacio had brought, everyone went to sleep to dream about finding Don Chipote.

18

Let's leave the family to rest and recuperate from the riotous journey, as we return to see what has happened to our friend, Don Chipote de Jesús María Domínguez.

As our readers will recall, our good buddy was going around with his head in the clouds, completely in love with a flapper who worked in a restaurant. You will not have forgotten that he went to see a witch doctor who would make a potion to win her love for him. And you will also remember that Don Chipote took out his loot and eventually handed it all over to said conjurer, trusting that two-bit hustler just like everyone else who gives him money.

Now we shall see if it helped our partner to obtain the object of his love.

There is a theater in Los Angeles where the hordes of Chicanos generally frequent and where the stage manager, who knows he has a gold mine, presents non-stop entertainment for the public's enjoyment.

One gimmick consists of raffling off furniture, money, and other more or less valuable objects to those who participate. Another gimmick is to invite amateurs, who think that they have a little talent, to dance, sing, recite poetry, walk the tightrope, or do whatever they know how to do. And there is a prize for the winner.

The love-struck men, who can't tell their girlfriends how they feel by way of reciting verse in the theater, will sing it to them. Others will use their windpipes to bellow out howl after howl for their girlfriends until their eyeballs turn all white. And so, this way, there is to-die-for entertainment every night, while the stage manager goes away with armloads of cash.

This is where Don Chipote liked to go: first, to express his love, and second, because he liked the show. One day, he decided he might be able to open his flapper up to him by inviting his beloved and going up on stage to sing to her. So he decided to give it a shot. And there you have it: Don Chipote rehearsing his song, reciting poetry, and breaking into the Charleston.

It was Wednesday, a day of much hubbub at that theater, when Don Chipote went and bought the tickets. And without beating around the bush, he invited his flapper girlfriend to accompany him to the show, which she agreed to do at once, without forcing him to beg.

Preparing to go up on stage and sing and recite, Don Chipote had bought himself a tuxedo, meaning his suit coat with little tails, as he called them. But since he hadn't bought the suit pants, he wore his bell-shaped slacks with the tuxedo jacket. The show finally got underway, and when the master of ceremonies asked those who would like to display their talents to come forward, Don Chipote, very determined, climbed up onto the stage to intone one of those songs from his *rancho* in which he told his mistress of his plan that, if she opened her heart to him, he would buy her percale petticoats and a shawl with little balls.

Since Don Chipote had taken a big swig of hooch before going onstage, he didn't feel embarrassed—or didn't know it if he did. And because what he wanted was to win over his flapper girlfriend, he sang the song with all his heart, winning five dollars as well as his respective Venus. This made Don Chipote feel like a true artist, and he decided to go up again when they called those who were going to recite poetry. Ah! But what he liked most was the soft touch that his flapper gave him.

The thrill of his theatrical triumph had not worn off Don Chipote when the announcer asked those who would like to enter the poetry recital to come forward, showing them a five-dollar bill as if dangling a carrot before a jackass. This motivated more than four guys to take to the stage, our partner among them. Now, not only did Don Chipote have the idea of showering his flapper with compliments, but he also believed that he could come away with the five semolians.

At the end of the night, after the show, he surrendered the five clams that he had won to the mistress of his loves and obtained her promise that, if he was able to be among the best and win the prize money again at next Wednesday's show, she would have to say yes to what he was after. Giving him a thunderous smack as a security deposit, the flapper took her leave of Don Chipote, who had become ecstatic and was seeing stars, for he never thought that he would be able to reach such exalted heights. So then, more in love now than ever before, he went to his room to dream about the pleasures that he would enjoy with his flapper. And because of this, he forgot all about his Chipote family and even started to think of himself as an eligible bachelor.

The next day, right after work, Don Chipote went to look for a bookstore which sold books of poetry and song lyrics, because he wanted to win the prize at all cost, as well as the mistress of his heart's love.

It didn't take him much effort to find what he wanted. And he began to search, right away, for someone to read them for him so that he could commit the songs to memory; as you may recall, the poor guy didn't know how to read. Because love conquers all, and because money talks, there was no lack of people willing to go over the lines of poetry with him, for a small fee, until he got them into his skull. The songs were more difficult, because the book didn't include the notes, making the book not worth a darn.

But, since love stimulates one's creativity, he went out and swallowed the drug of the phonograph and its respective records. Among them were the songs which truly touched his soul, and which, according to him, were capable of moving even the hardest-hearted woman. So he believed that the lyrics to *"Limoncito," "El carretero," "Las coplas de Don Simón,"* and others of the like, were the very keys to open his flapper's heart.

Only those who lived in the same house as Don Chipote could describe the pain he inflicted upon them during the days he spent learning the songs. But, so that you better understand, understand that from the moment he arrived home from work until the moment he surrendered to sleep, Don Chipote was playing the phonograph and listening to the same song, over and over again. After the phonograph stopped, he continued to sing at the top of his lungs to see if he knew it yet. And that's how, giving it his all and annoying everyone in the neighborhood, he managed to stick two songs and two poems into his coconut, which, according to him, would get him carried off on the shoulders of the audience after his triumph on the day of the contest, to later hear the long-awaited "yes" that he had been carrying around in his head for so long but had not been able to obtain, not even with the love potion made by the sorcerer for that exact purpose.

The long-awaited Wednesday arrived at last, and with it Don Chipote's invitation to his flapper girlfriend to go and see his next triumph on the stage. She accepted his invitation. And when the time came, they went arm-in-arm right to the front row seats.

Let's go back again to see what has happened to the Chipote family: The day after they arrived in Los Angeles, they had to check out of the hotel, because the kids made such a ruckus that the manager asked them to take a hike. All of the other guests had threatened to vacate their rooms if the family did not leave the hotel, because the Chipote children had not let anyone sleep all night with their screaming and crying.

Pitacio hit the road very early to find somewhere else to stay, which he was able to locate after wandering around all morning and afternoon. They changed living quarters to a tiny house very close to the Placita, the owners fully aware that their renters had a gang of little brats who raised more Cain than the devil himself.

The days went by, and, both Pitacio and Doña Chipota occupied themselves with investigating Don Chipote's whereabouts. But for all their inquiries, nobody could provide any information.

On the day of the show when Don Chipote planned to demonstrate his artistic talents for the second time in, honor of his beloved torment, Doña Chipota also wanted at last to have a little fun. Passing by the theater, having looked for her husband in vain for hours, she was convinced by the announcer to go inside, along with her flock, to have a good time. And without further ado, she bought the tickets and went into the theater for the first time.

All was swell during the presentation of the movie. As her children laughed their heads off watching the picture show, Doña Chipota felt very happy to have spent the money to go inside and enjoy herself.

The variety show then followed. But Doña Chipota didn't understand what was going on. In fact, she disliked it so much that she almost fell asleep as the little ones snored soundly.

Then came the much-anticipated moment in which spectators climb up on the stage. At the call of the guy with the baton, a few started into the dance competition to win themselves a prize. All of the goings-on made such a racket that the flock of Chipotes woke up and peeled back their eyes to enjoy the buffoonery of those who went up. Meanwhile, Don Chipote was pulling his hair out, thinking that he had not learned a dance for the competition, since he could have won the prize that way too.

The moment of truth finally arrived in which the Chicanos were called to compete for the prize in singing. And without waiting for an, "On your mark, get set, go," Don Chipote raced to the front and was the first to take to the stage.

Doña Chipota recognized Don Chipote as soon as she saw him. A scream escaped from her trap at the same time that Pitacio shouted, "Looky there! That's my pal!" And all the little squirts, in unison, shouted, "That's my *papá!*"

Since he couldn't hear anything over the noise of the audience, Don Chipote didn't realize that he had been spotted and started to sing.

In the meantime, Doña Chipota had gotten up from her seat and made a run for the front of the stage. There, with no courtesy whatsoever, she went up to Don Chipote and attacked him with slaps in the face, all the while saying, "Shame on you! Bad husband! Comin' here all fancied up an' cattin' 'round while we're starvin' ta death. But I gotcha now. An' now you're a gonna see what'll happen ta ya. C'mon. You're a comin' with me so's you kin he'p me carry the lil' uns an' stop horsin' 'round wit' all this nonsense." And she clobbered him with a good one to the face.

As she turned away, Don Chipote, still stunned, ran after his wife and took hold of Doña Chipota, who then began wringing his neck like a chicken's.

As our readers can imagine, this number was not in the program. And it was a real surprise for the audience. With thunderous applause, they demanded the prize be awarded to those who so brilliantly portrayed the comedy of husband and wife.

Don Chipote continued to run circles around his spouse, unable to evade the walloping that she was giving him.

The crowd laughed like crazy, still convinced that it was just a gag to win the five dollars. But when the flock of little Chipotitos made their appearance on stage and embraced their father from all sides, and he stopped restraining Doña Chipota for the love of his children, the audience asked for them to be sent to jail.

The theater had already made a call to the cops. In less than the blink of an eye, the whole Chipote family was sitting in the paddy-wagon on its way to the joint, where, without going into any formalities, they were deposited in their respective departments so that they could await whatever the judge might tell them the following day.

Poor Doña Chipota and the entire herd of little Chipotitos were placed in the department for women. Seeing herself in such a fix, she didn't want her cheese any more, but only to get out of the mousetrap. So she put her faith in the Eleven Thousand Virgins to save her and all of the Chipotes from such a predicament. The little Chipotitos cried for a little while, but since they had their mother close by, they soon closed their eyes. Not the good lady, who cried all night with snot dangling from her nose.

As for Don Chipote and Pitacio, these cocks were thrown into the cockpit, where they didn't exchange words for a very long time, frightened as they were and unable to collect themselves. At last, after a long silence, Don Chipote gave signs of life and asked Pitacio if he were asleep, to which he said no and that as punishment for his sins, he was locked up with Don Chipote, his children, and his wife, to help pay for his evil deeds.

Hearing this, Don Chipote asked him at once to tell him why he had brought the lady. Without wasting any time, Pitacio sang like a stool pigeon and told Don Chipote that it was all his fault. Not waiting for further explanation, Don Chipote jumped on top of Pitacio and beat him into pulp. Not to be outdone, Pitacio answered back. In a few minutes the two were bleeding from the nose and mouth, and their eyes were as black as crows'. But that didn't stop them from belting each other some more.

Like good Mexicans, as much Don Chipote as Pitacio, they surely would have pulled out each other's eyebrows with the quarreling that they were carrying on, if it were not for a pair of cops who brutishly fished them out of their cell by the bands of their underwear and threw them into separate tanks.

Once apart, and without the comfort of seeing the condition of the other one, they fumed in their respective bunks. And, banged up from all of the ruckus, they hit the sack and put themselves to dreaming.

As soon as Don Chipote—who by the looks of him was beat up to the point of saying "uncle"—closed his eyes, he began to dream about his flapper girlfriend. And in the dream, it looked liked they were on a honeymoon. He told her sweet nothings and ran his fingers through her hair. Then, suddenly, his dream changed, and he saw his happiness cut short by the presence of a witch, who, envious of his love, changed him into a mule with one slap. He no longer puckered his lips, but hee-hawed until he finally woke up, feeling the whipping that Pitacio had given him.

For Pitacio's part, he also began to dream the moment he started to snore. Only his dreams were sweeter, because he saw himself dressed like his friend Don Chipote, in bell-shaped trousers and a tail coat and painting the town red. On Main Street, all his fellow countrymen hailed him as a man of distinction. He, too, saw the flappers whom, when awake, he had admired so much. They followed after him and they begged him to take them by the arm, to which he acted indifferently. In the end, as he strutted like a peacock and paid no attention to where he was going, a car came and ran him over like a bump in the road. A very long horn blast was heard, and he felt himself being transported by an enormous bird. He awoke, thinking that the doctors were shaking him from side to side to cure him of his injuries, but found out that it was just a flatfoot who called him to go stand before the judge for sentencing.

As our readers will see, the time for police consultation had arrived. Pitacio was the first to appear before the judge to testify to the charge of disturbing the peace.

Pitacio answered the questions the judge directed to him with the truth, the whole truth, and nothing but the truth. And he would have certainly gone free, if it had not occurred to the judge to ask him for his passport. Since Pitacio didn't give a satisfactory response, nor could he produce the document, because he didn't have one, the judge pulled the story out of him like a corkscrew: how he and all the Chipote family had entered—that is to say, were smuggled—into the United States. With this, he was set aside so that immigration officials could come for him later.

Don Chipote immediately followed. He was dragged over the coals by the judge and also sang like a bird about all of his adventures, for which he too was set aside.

Doña Chipota and the little Chipotitos came immediately after. And this was the last nail in the coffin, Doña Chipota telling the judge how she had come in search of her husband, who, for all she knew, was whooping it up with all the gals in the United States.

With Doña Chipota's declaration, there was no other resolution possible for the case. Without hearing any more accounts, the judge dispatched them to the immigration officers to do with them as the law requires in such cases.

Upon seeing that the case was lost, the family made peace and came to an agreement to see if they could save themselves from whatever might happen next.

What did happen was that the police transferred them to the Big House, where they keep those who have committed major offenses. So, all of them, tied to a cop like beads on a necklace, reached a hotel which looked like a palace to them. Never in their lives had they set foot inside such a gigantic mansion. In the end, they were thrilled to have arrived at chow time. And because they hadn't eaten since the previous night, they eagerly dove into whatever Fate had placed before them.

It would be useless to report what happened to them in prison, because it is commonly known that the Chicano community finds the worst in whatever part of the United States they find themselves. We'll just say that they were found guilty of violating the immigration laws and sentenced to deportation.

19

One day when they least expected it and had already begun to take a liking to their hotel, they were told to pack their bags to ship out for their homeland.

This announcement was received differently by each person. While it fell on Pitacio like a ton of bricks, for the others, if they were not thrilled, at least they weren't upset.

As for Doña Chipota, she was so excited that she almost rolled on the floor. After all, what she wanted was to be with her husband, and not in the United States, but on their *rancho,* where she would delight in the scorching heat.

Don Chipote did go pale indeed when he heard the news. Not because he didn't want to go back to his fatherland, but because his heart still yearned for his flapper love, whom, from the look of things, he would have to renounce forever. Likewise, he thought about poor Skinenbones, who, abandoned by his owners on the day of their arrest, would probably be starving to death in the hotel room where they had left him locked up. This broke his heart, considering the mistreatment his friend and companion in adventure had received as a reward for his loyalty. What Don Chipote did not know was that his faithful pet was found enjoying the best part of life. Having been able to escape from the room, he was run over by a streetcar while wandering through the streets looking for his masters. This left him dead on the spot.

Pitacio, for his part, regretted the deportation most. He hadn't stopped grieving from the moment he heard the sentence, complaining that he had suffered through all of Doña Chipota's temper tantrums for nothing, because he had paid too high a price.

The day finally arrived when they had to ship out—or better said, when they were shipped out. They were picked up very early and loaded into an automobile which carried them pell-mell to the Southern Pacific Railroad Station.

In no time at all, they were packed into one of those railroad cars that is always about to take off. In a few moments, and always accompanied by the immigration police, they left the City of Angels for their native soil.

What happened on the way is of little importance, for there were no events of interest. Almost without exchanging a word, everyone was absorbed in their own thoughts. Those thoughts, one might say, transported them more quickly than the train they were taking.

I can only tell you of Don Chipote that, for all the distance his body was separated from Los Angeles, his heart stayed back with his flapper girlfriend and ill-fated dog.

Arriving in El Paso, Texas, they were herded to the International Bridge, where, with much pushing and shoving, they were thrown into their homeland, bedbugs and all.

As soon as they crossed the bridge, they went uphill to a shade tree and gave free rein to their remorse. They would have spent the entire night there, too, if it were not for Doña Chipota, who, like all Mexican women, was mistrustful of her surroundings and for the whole time had carried all her remaining dough in tightly knotted piece of cloth hidden in her bosom.

They weren't broke, then.

Don Chipote, for his part, also had a few clams, because the night that the old battle-ax caught up to him, he had asked the restaurant for an advance so he could take his flapper to the theater. And since he had spent only for the tickets, he had about four and a half semolians.

As soon as Doña Chipota eyeballed the stash her husband had, she snatched it away from him, her pretext being that she was the one who had to attend to the family's needs. Don Chipote, his tail between his legs, didn't argue.

In total, after counting and recounting their loot, the family found itself with the sum of thirty-three dollars, which, exchanged, came to about seventy pesos.

Since the question of food was foremost on their minds, they first went to the market. With the best of intentions, they circled around a *menudo* stand, which, after a short while, they left looking like a tornado had hit it, as did the guy who was selling the corn tortillas.

Then they found a place to spend the night.

The following day, a Chipote family meeting was called, a meeting in which no one had a say except Doña Chipota. They agreed to undertake the long walk to the home of their birth. But Pitacio chose instead to remain in Ciudad Juárez to see what Fate had in store for him.

Once this matter had been resolved, Don Chipote was authorized to purchase a pair of mules as cheaply as possible, which he quickly accomplished. So, for forty eagle-faced pesos, he got a couple of donkeys which were of good use, though somewhat scrawny.

They then bought some baskets to accommodate the little Chipotitos as well as the ball-and-chain. And they prepared themselves for the trip as best they could.

On the eve of their departure, Don Chipote requested and received a gift from his wife: a pair of pants, so that he wouldn't ruin his bell-shaped slacks and his suit coat with tails.

Once this was taken care of, they spent their last night in Ciudad Juárez hoping to go home as soon as possible. The next day, very early in the morning, after asking the Virgin Mary to deliver them safely, the five left well-equipped. They embarked upon the long journey towards the end of their adventures.

It would be pointless to describe what happened to the members of the Chipote family, because you can already imagine what transpired, considering the things that they brought along for the trip.

I only know to tell you that during their voyage, by way of Don Chipote's affection for his spouse, he was able to win back Doña Chipota's trust, and she forgave him *in saecula saeculorum.*

And that's how, in blessed harmony, after painstaking days, they spied the spires of the chapel where they had soaked their heads in baptism. The joy that came over them is beyond description. To give thanks to the Virgin Mary for the miracle of delivering them safely to their beloved home, they kneeled and spewed from their mouths a few prayers that they had learned when they were children.

Then, their hearts overflowing with gaiety, they proceeded forward until reaching their rickety old *rancho.* Abandoned, it was in disastrous condition, for it had been overrun by the neighbors' animals, which happily trampled the pasture.

The arrival of the Chipote clan was quite an event for the neighbors and family. They even fought among themselves to help them in some way, believing that, because they had gone to the United States, the Chipotes had brought back big bags full of dough. This was something the Chipotes were careful not to confirm or deny, knowing that if they told the truth and confessed their penury, everyone would stop helping them and throwing parties for them.

The first day was spent attending to their visitors, for whom Don Chipote put on his long slacks and tail coat. The next day passed in cleaning the house and finding things to fill it with, because what Doña Chipota hadn't sold, she had given away on shoving off in search of her husband. The third day, Don Chipote, dragging one of his donkeys while riding the other, went to see his old *patrón* to see if he could get some work.

He got what he hoped for from said *patrón*—that is, he received a few parcels to plant in halves, and he was also able to sell the *patrón* one of his donkeys for cash expenses until the harvest came in.

20
Epilogue

The sun vanished into the twilight as the clouds cloaked themselves in rouge upon receiving the last caress from the blanket of the poor. And like a lady of the night, the clouds changed from scarlet, to pale, to darkness, resembling the black eyes of starving clowns.

Loving flocks, gathered in their nests, gave welcoming pecks, fluffed their wings, and prepared to snore.

Bumblebees ceased buzzing and puckered up, preparing to pass the night. Honeybees returned to the hive to puke up the honey they had swallowed. And the brook continued to sing and run its course while soaking the roots of the *camichime* and *zalate* trees.

All was peace and calm. All nature entered into a state of rest, except for Don Chipote, who, completely worn out from the daily grind, continued to poke at his oxen's asses. So obliged by his numerous progeny, he was forced to bring up the rear of his horny beasts, occasionally sucking in the consoling little emanations from the animals' posterior ducts.

And all the while, he dreamt . . . . And in his dreams he saw bitter adventures, in which he had played the protagonist, unwind like a movie reel, sweetened by the remembrance of his flapper's love. It was a memory that would not allow him to forget the troubles that Chicanos experience when leaving their fatherland, made starry-eyed by the yarns spun by those who go to the United States, as they say, to strike it rich.

And pondering all of this, he came to the conclusion that Mexicans will make it big in the United States . . . WHEN PARROTS BREAST-FEED.